"Say that again! About dating."

"What?" he asked idly.

"You know. That if I was seeing anybody at all, the well-meaning busybodies would smile and stay out of my life."

"Is that what I said?" Now he sounded amused.

"And I wouldn't *really* have to be seeing anyone, as long as they all thought I was."

"Don't you think the phantom lover would be a tough act to pull off?"

Rachel chewed on her bottom lip. "I suppose that's true. But if there was someone who understood..."

"You mean someone who's in the same boat, I suppose? Lady, if you're talking about me..."

Rachel blinked in surprise. "I wasn't. But now that you mention it..."

Leigh Michaels has always enjoyed Thanksgiving, and usually the holiday finds at least fifteen gathered to enjoy her gourmet turkey (the two secrets, she says, are lots of basting, and roasting in a 400-degree oven for the first hour to achieve a nice brown skin, then reducing the temperature to 325 degrees till the bird is done). But the holiday took on extra meaning for her recently, when her cousin discovered that they are direct descendants of Francis Cooke, a *Mayflower* passenger who took part in the very first Thanksgiving celebration in North America.

Dating Games is the fifth and final McKenna story featured in Harlequin Romance. It follows #3010—*No Place Like Home,* #3070—*A Matter of Principal,* #3171—*Garrett's Back in Town,* and #3233—*The Unexpected Landlord.*

Books by Leigh Michaels

HARLEQUIN ROMANCE
3184—OLD SCHOOL TIES
3214—THE BEST MADE PLANS
3233—THE UNEXPECTED LANDLORD
3248—SAFE IN MY HEART
3263—TIES THAT BLIND
3275—THE LAKE EFFECT

DATING GAMES
Leigh Michaels

Harlequin Books

TORONTO • NEW YORK • LONDON
AMSTERDAM • PARIS • SYDNEY • HAMBURG
STOCKHOLM • ATHENS • TOKYO • MILAN
MADRID • WARSAW • BUDAPEST • AUCKLAND

For my cousin Sheryl Hayden,
who found our *Mayflower* line.

ISBN 0-373-03290-0

DATING GAMES

CHAPTER ONE

IT WAS SUCH A PERFECT Indian-summer morning that on the spur of the moment Rachel decided to walk to work. The October breeze was just crisp enough to make her glad she'd pulled her new wool suit out of the closet this morning. But the sun was shining, giving an extra glitter to the red and gold and yellow of the trees lining the quiet residential streets of Lakemont.

The few leaves that had already fallen made a satisfying crunch beneath Rachel's feet. Another floated down from a maple tree as she passed and alighted in her hair, a bright yellow accent against her dark copper curls.

On a lawn nearby, half a dozen children had scraped together a big pile of leaves, and they were jumping into it with abandon. For one instant, Rachel thought about joining them, but then she shook her head with a smile. It would be difficult enough for the children to explain their dusty and disheveled condition when they got to school. For Rachel it would be impossible. Serious professional women didn't do that sort of thing.

At least not until *after* work, she thought. And not while wearing a brand-new suit.

She turned a corner and stepped onto the campus of Nicolet University. The glorious range of color lining the quadrangle brought a nostalgic lump to her throat.

It felt good to be back where there were honest-to-goodness seasons, Rachel thought. She'd missed seeing the slow progress of each year, from the breathless hush before spring burst forth in a tender green haze, through lush summer and brilliant autumn. . . .

"And into frigid winter," she muttered. "We'll see just how nostalgic you're feeling in a couple of months, when the snow is knee-deep and the wind howls down from the Arctic. You'll probably wish yourself back in Arizona then."

But the flash of self-mocking good humor gave way a moment later to a flood of bleak memory. Nothing, she thought, would ever make her go back to Arizona.

That wasn't fair. It wasn't the whole state that had been the problem, after all—just a couple of its inhabitants.

She heard someone shouting her name and swung around abruptly. From half a block away a woman in a plaid jacket waved and hurried to catch up.

Dawn Morgan must have an early class to teach, Rachel mused. She retraced her steps to meet her.

Dawn was out of breath. "What's on your mind this morning, Rachel? I've been calling and running to catch up, but you didn't seem to hear."

"Sorry. I was just admiring the colors."

"It is beautiful, isn't it?" Dawn fell into step beside Rachel, shuffling her feet through the rustling layer of leaves on the sidewalk. "I just hope the weather holds for another two weeks, 'till Fall Festival. It's so late this year there may not be a leaf left on the trees by that time."

"What would happen then? No festival?"

"Hardly. Cancel the Fall Festival and you'd give up Nicolet University's biggest celebration of the year. No matter what, there'll be a festival. And you'll love it."

Rachel shrugged. "It's just another street carnival, isn't it?"

Dawn laughed. "Trust me. It can't be described or explained, it can only be experienced. And you can't truly be a part of Nicolet until you've attended it." She darted a glance at Rachel. "What are you planning to do this weekend?"

"I'm going to put up bookshelves in my living room. Why?"

Dawn's eyes brightened. "I hope you found a good-looking carpenter."

I ought to have seen that coming, Rachel thought. "Don't you start on me, too," she said plaintively. "Isn't it bad enough that my boss has a nephew she thinks would be perfect for me? I have to work with the woman, so I can hardly tell her I'd rather be boiled in oil than date Gerald. But if my friends start matchmaking, too..."

Dawn laughed. "Well, you must admit you're a challenge. You've been at Nicolet four months now, and from all appearances you haven't even met any interesting men. If you were doing something about it yourself..."

"Of course I've met interesting men. For instance, Ted Lehmann. I spent several hours with him last week when we flew to Minneapolis for that conference on student financial services, and I—"

"President Lehmann doesn't count. He's fifty-three and he has six grandchildren, and if he left his wife to take up with the assistant director of financial aid, the whole university would grind to a halt."

"Dawn, if you meant *eligible* men, you shouldn't have said *interesting*."

"You knew perfectly well what I meant."

"I am not looking for a man." Rachel's tone was firm. Too firm, perhaps, as she saw Dawn's eyes narrow suspiciously. Rachel let a note of laughter creep into her voice. "I don't need a man, anyway. I can put up my own bookshelves. A few boards and brackets, a screwdriver, a drill... Who needs a carpenter?"

"I'm all for self-sufficiency. And nobody says you have to get serious. But with Fall Festival coming up and everything..."

"I know what's going on." Rachel snapped her fingers. "You're suffering from a disease, Dawn. When you're newly engaged, it's natural to think everyone else in the world should be part of a twosome, as well, but you'll get over it with time. Just take two aspirins and—"

"All right," Dawn said. "I give up. I'll leave you to the fond interference of your boss. Maybe Gerald won't be so bad, after all."

Rachel shuddered. "Don't make a joke of it. Last week I couldn't come up with a plausible excuse, and I ended up having coffee with Gerald."

"That bad, hmm?"

"Worse."

"Well, it doesn't mean all the men in Lakemont are losers. Jason has a new friend at work—"

"I thought you were going to give it up, Dawn."

Dawn didn't seem to hear. "I'll ask Jason if his friend would like to come to Fall Festival with us and make a foursome. It's really not the same without a date."

Rachel stopped on the bottom step of the flight leading up to the administration building and looked down at her friend. "I'd tell you I appreciate the except I don't, Dawn. I have a job that keeps busy, and I have all sorts of friends to keep me company. Or at least I will have as long as they don't drive me crazy setting up blind dates. You haven't forgotten your class, have you?"

Dawn gasped, looked at her wristwatch and wheeled around toward the liberal-arts hall. But she took a moment for a final over-the-shoulder jab. "Nobody's suggesting you ought to get married by next week, Rachel. But it wouldn't hurt just to have some fun!"

Rachel shook her head in rueful amusement and climbed the rest of the steps to her office in the financial-aid wing. It took so little to make Dawn happy, she thought. It was too bad, really, that her appointment for lunch today was only a business engagement and that the person she was meeting was female. The pleasure of telling Dawn she had a date would almost have been worth the cross-examination.

THE PACE in the financial-aid office of a major university never really let up, and in her four months on the job, Rachel had discovered that Nicolet University was busier than most. Not only was it a prestigious institution, but private and ruinously expensive, which meant that most of the students needed some form of assistance to help pay for their education. October, when applications started to come in for money for the following academic year, was shaping up to be a particularly hectic month.

By noon, Rachel was convinced she'd talked to half the students on campus. She left her desk just as the telephone began to ring once more, feeling a bit guilty about not answering the caller. Still, if she didn't simply walk out, she'd never get away.

"I'm leaving this madhouse," she told her secretary, "to have lunch with Mrs. Garrett and discuss some changes in the journalism-school scholarship programs. So when the other half of the student body starts calling, just tell everyone I'll be unavailable for a couple of hours.'

"That sounds like heartfelt relief," said a dark-haired young woman who got up from the waiting area, folding a lightweight coat over her arm.

"Anne!" Rachel wheeled around to face her. "I didn't see you there."

"I'd hoped it was my shimmering personality that made you sound so eager to have lunch with me, but obviously—"

"Why didn't you let me know you were waiting?"

"And keep you from enjoying your job for a few extra minutes?" Anne Garrett shook her head. "I was early, anyway. I had a meeting at the journalism school that miraculously didn't take longer than scheduled. Is the student-union restaurant all right, or would you like to shake the dust of the campus off your feet altogether?"

"The union's fine." It was silly to have twinges about whether Anne might have misunderstood her frustration. True, Anne Garrett was not a woman to be taken lightly. She was not only involved in the new journalism scholarship program, she was the assistant publisher of the Lakemont *Chronicle,* the largest single source of financial support Nicolet University had. And she was also one of the nicest people Rachel had met in her four months on the job.

As they nabbed the last available table in the student grill, Rachel said, "The office has been like a crisis hot line this morning. The financial-aid packets went out a month ago, but everybody on campus must have waited till today to look at the forms. The phones have been ringing off the hook."

Anne smiled. "I've had moments like that at the newspaper. Sometimes that kind of day is enough to make you wonder if the last promotion was worth it, isn't it?"

Rachel nodded. "Either that, or really look forward to the next one." She'd already figured out some of the new directions she would take as director of the financial-aid office, should her supervisor retire. For starters, she'd create clearer instructions on how to fill out the forms. . . .

The retirement of the current director would also mean she wouldn't have Gerald thrust at her anymore.

Anne opened her menu. "Are the Reuben sandwiches here still as good as they used to be?"

"I'm not the right one to ask," Rachel pointed out, "since I have no idea how good they used to be."

"Sorry. You've fit so naturally into the office and the university that it's hard to believe you've only been here a few months." They each ordered a Reuben, and Anne went on, "Have you had a chance to meet many people yet?"

"Quite a few. It's easier to get acquainted at a university, of course, since everyone's come here from somewhere else. The environment is more open to newcomers."

Anne nodded. "People here are more willing to be sociable with strangers, without asking a lot of probing questions."

She'd hit the nail on the head. "Exactly. I don't have much time to socialize, though."

"Your predecessor left things in a mess, did he?"

"Yes, but it's not entirely that. Once I'm settled in the job, I'm going to start taking some classes again."

Anne stopped stirring her iced tea. "My dear girl, you've already got—what? Three degrees?"

"Just two."

"Oh, well, in that case, of course you need another." Anne gave her an elfin grin. "Do you think you could carve out a little time on Saturday evening to come to dinner?"

An invitation to dinner from the Garrett family—no matter how casually it was phrased—wasn't the kind of opportunity a second-level administrator turned down, even if it hadn't sounded like fun. "I'd like that," she said.

"Good. Seven o'clock. Our house, in Pemberton Place..." Anne paused and leaned back to let the student waiter put her plate down. "Is there someone you'd like to bring? Otherwise, I can just have my extra male guest stop by to pick you up."

Not her, too, Rachel thought in dismay. With an effort, she kept her voice light. "Why is there such a passion around Nicolet for matchmaking? Everyone seems to have an idea for pairing me off."

"I suppose it's the Fall Festival," Anne said mildly. "Everyone seems to be paired up for it. And then of course there's the weather. Once fall sets in, we all start thinking about cuddling up with a warm body in front of the fireplace...."

"That's why I have a cat."

Anne smiled. "Still," she murmured, "as clumsy as I must have sounded, matchmaking wasn't what I had in mind at all. Formal dinners, you know... I was only asking in the hope of balancing my table and keeping the numbers even.''

Rachel bit her lip. Good heavens, she thought. You're becoming so sensitive you're seeing trouble where it doesn't even exist.

She said weakly, ''Oh. I'm very sorry. How rude of me to assume—'' She stopped and tried again. ''Just because everyone else seems ...''

Anne nodded wisely. ''Dorie Lehmann has started on you, I suppose?''

''The president's wife?'' Rachel's voice was a squeak of surprise.

''She hasn't? She'll get around to it.''

Rachel cut her Reuben in half and muttered, ''I just wish everyone would leave me alone.''

''To find love in your own way?'' The words sounded a bit melodramatic, but the tone was sympathetic.

Rachel almost nodded, but at the last instant something pushed her to tell the truth. ''No. I'd like to avoid the situation altogether. But no one seems to believe I am simply not interested in capturing a man.'' Surely, she told herself, Anne Garrett wouldn't be shocked by that. As a professional woman herself, she certainly couldn't believe that no woman could be complete without a husband ... could she?

''That must be very frustrating. Perhaps if you weren't quite so militantly opposed to the idea, people might mind their own business. They do sometimes.'' Anne took a bite of her sandwich and smiled. ''Yes, it's as good as I remembered. We'll have to do this more often. Now, what about the scholarship program, Rachel? I thought we had it all worked out.''

Rachel seized on the topic, happy to have the subject of her love life put aside. "It's nothing major, but now that the program is a couple of years old, there are a few little bugs turning up—things that might toss out some well-qualified candidates. It almost always happens, no matter how carefully a program has been planned. For instance..."

IT TOOK MOST of their two-hour lunch to plan a new strategy for the journalism-school scholarship, and Rachel spent the afternoon getting the details down on paper. She stayed late, after the telephones stopped ringing, to finish up the rest of her work for the day, and she was just closing the final folder when the rain began.

Huge drops pelted the windows of her office like fists, and Rachel looked up with a groan. She hadn't noticed, sitting inside her artificially lighted cocoon, that as evening approached the sky had grown particularly dark and gloomy. She'd been concentrating so hard she hadn't even heard the rumble of thunder. So here she was, stuck with no transportation, the rest of the office employees already gone, with not even a raincoat and wearing a new wool suit...

"Which will be soaked and starting to shrink by the time I walk the eight blocks home," she muttered.

In a closet tucked under the administration building's old wooden stairs, she found a faded pink polka-dot umbrella with two broken ribs. She had her doubts about how it would hold up, but it was better than nothing. She opened it cautiously and stepped out into the rain.

This was no pleasant little shower, she quickly realized. The raindrops were cold, and they hit her nylon-clad legs with the force of pebbles flung by an angry child.

She crossed the street in front of the building, hoping that the row of retail shops across from the campus would provide more shelter. But just as she stepped onto the curb again, the clouds burst and her umbrella collapsed. She headed for the nearest doorway with her head bent, almost blinded by the sudden downpour.

Once inside, Rachel tried to shake the rain off as she looked around the packed ice-cream parlor. Old wooden booths lined the walls. In the center of the room was a collection of antique wrought-iron chairs and marble-topped tables. And lined up in a row behind the stainless-steel soda fountain was the most garish collection of modern neon sculptures Rachel had ever seen.

It could be worse, she told herself. She could have landed in an adults-only bookstore. Still, the thought of ice cream on a day like this was hardly comforting.

She glanced out at the sidewalk. Normally at this hour the streets around campus were busy, but now there were only a few passersby, figures bent against the rain. One man, his head protected by a newspaper, looked up just as he passed the lighted window where Rachel stood, and for an instant she thought it was her supervisor's nephew. "Not Gerald," she muttered. "Oh, please, don't let it be Gerald!"

The man showed not a hint of recognition, however, and Rachel made her way to the back of the ice-cream parlor and sank weakly into the only empty booth.

Her attitude was getting to be ridiculous, she told herself. Gerald might be a bore, but he wasn't stupid; eventually he would take the hint that Rachel wasn't particularly interested in him. There was no need to panic about the situation.

It was several minutes before a waitress in a perky pink candy-striped uniform came by to take her order. Rachel asked for a cup of hot chocolate and wished she had a towel to wipe the raindrops off her ankles.

I should have just stayed at work, she thought. At least I'd still be dry, and I could have accomplished something useful there.

The family in the next booth rose to leave, and two young men took their place. Rachel thought one of them seemed a bit familiar, but she didn't get a good look at him because the waitress delivered her hot chocolate just then. She stirred it morosely till the marshmallows melted, then took a sip.

Maybe she'd start on those bookshelves tonight—if the rain let up so she could manage to get home. If she got the shelves sanded, it would help speed the job on Saturday. Otherwise, she might not get finished before it was time to go to Anne Garrett's dinner party.

Pemberton Place, she mused. A nice neighborhood, one of the oldest and most elegant in the city. Even newcomers to Lakemont soon heard about Pemberton Place...

Suddenly she realized she'd forgotten to ask Anne for the precise address, thrown off as she'd been by all the discussion about matchmaking. She also hadn't made it clear she didn't need assistance to get to the party.

I'll have to call her, Rachel thought, or the extra man will show up on my doorstep Saturday night, after all. And in that case, she would end up spending the evening with the worst sort of blind date—one who was paying attention to her only because he owed his hostess a favor. It was not a formula for a successful evening.

Rachel groaned. The whole thing was getting out of hand.

What was it Dawn had said? "You're a challenge," that was it. "If you were doing something about it yourself..."

But I don't want to do anything about it, Rachel thought rebelliously. I certainly don't want to date. I'm always going to be independent, so why should I waste time when I could be doing something worthwhile?

There was a time, of course, when she had felt differently, when she thought she had found the one man in the world who was right for her. But that had been before...

The bleakness settled over her again like a smothering blanket. The pain came less frequently these days, but in a way it was almost worse now than when it had been her constant companion. Just when she began to think that perhaps it wouldn't come back again at all, she found it lying in ambush in the corners of her mind.

Her hand trembled on her mug. Deliberately she focused her mind on things outside herself—the child at a nearby table who was slurping a cherry cola, the waitress's incredibly impractical high heels, the conversation in the next booth....

"You have got to do something about your wife." It was one of the men from the next booth, and there was an edge to his tone, something between frustration and annoyance, that she found fascinating.

Too bad I'm not into writing mystery novels, she thought. I think I've just stumbled across a plot!

"Pregnant women are supposed to draw into themselves, Patrick," the man went on. "They shouldn't have dreamy thoughts about anything but pickles and ice cream—"

His companion interrupted him. "Why do you think I suggested we meet here, anyway? I've got orders to bring home a quart of chocolate almond fudge for her."

"—and pink-and-blue wallpaper," the first man went on ruthlessly. "But this particular pregnant woman seems to think she's a dating service with one client. Me."

Rachel lost interest. Same old stuff, she thought. Though she supposed it ought to make her feel better to know that other people had the same problems with matchmakers as she had.

She finished her hot chocolate and paid the bill. The storm did not appear to be letting up; sheets of water were still hitting the front windows of the ice-cream parlor, and in the street outside ankle-deep streams were running. She stood with one hand on the door, holding the useless umbrella, and wondered if it was possible to get a cab at this hour.

She was so absorbed in watching the rain that she wasn't aware of anyone else trying to leave the shop until a man's voice said, "Excuse me."

Rachel jumped guiltily away from the door as if he'd demanded she get out of his way.

Only then did he really seem to see her. "You're Miss Todd, aren't you?" he said. It was the voice she'd overheard from the next booth—the man who'd been complaining about the other's wife.

Startled, she stared up at him. He might have been thirty, with eyes the color of a summer sky, wide-set and fringed with ridiculously long and curly dark lashes. His almost-black hair was in need of cutting, and it looked windblown....

The resemblance that had nagged at her when he'd first come in snapped into place. "You're Ted Lehmann's pilot," she said. "You flew us to Minneapolis last week."

It was not surprising she hadn't recognized him before. The cabin arrangement of the ten-passenger turboprop wouldn't have allowed her to admire the pilot's profile even if she *had* been so inclined. But she did remember the clipped voice in which the pilot had issued safety instructions, and the way he'd had to bend his head in the less-than-roomy cabin. She also remembered the butter-smooth takeoffs and landings.

He smiled a little. "Well, I'm not exactly Ted's private property." He paused. "Are you meeting someone?"

"No. It was so beautiful this morning that I left my car at home. And now..."

"You're waiting for the rain to stop? I hope you've got a sleeping bag." He zipped up his leather jacket. "Once it starts to rain around here it can go on for days."

"It's nice of you to be so encouraging, Mr.—"

"I'll give you a ride home if you like."

His companion turned away from the cash register and came toward the door, folding the top of an insulated paper bag. The two men had the same coloring, she noticed, though this one was a few inches shorter. And a few years older—or was that just the conservative cut of his clothes and hair? He nodded politely at Rachel as he buttoned his trench coat and then said to the man beside her, "I wouldn't worry about Camryn anymore."

Rachel watched the younger man's eyes light up. "You'll tell her to lay off?"

The older man smiled at Rachel. "Not quite," he said gently. "I'll tell her you're doing just fine on your own." The door swung shut behind him.

Rachel looked up at the man beside her and was startled to see a reddish flush creeping into his cheeks. He needn't be embarrassed for my sake, she thought. Or was it that he was afraid she'd take his companion's comment as encouragement?

"Matchmaking friends?" she said crisply.

He sighed. "Family. Sisters-in-law, to be precise. I've got three of them and they're driving me crazy."

"I know the feeling." So that had been his brother. No wonder their coloring was so similar.

There was undoubted interest in his eyes. "You, too?"

Rachel nodded. "People think there's something weird about a woman who doesn't want to date. I'd love a ride home, if the offer's still open. Otherwise, I suppose this town has a taxi service, doesn't it?"

"Not much of one. You could be here for hours. Come on. My car's right across the street."

The vehicle he indicated was not quite old enough to be considered an antique, but it was close, and Rachel looked at it doubtfully. The interior, however, was meticulously clean, and the engine started with a throaty eagerness she found reassuring. Besides, she thought, anybody who flew an airplane could surely keep a car running with one hand tied behind his back.

"It brings out the very worst in people, doesn't it?" he said as the car nosed out onto the rain-slick street.

"Hmm?"

"Matchmaking."

"Oh, absolutely. Some of the combinations people suggest, and with a perfectly straight face...." She lapsed into a thoughtful silence. "You know," she said almost to herself, "somebody gave me a bit of advice just today about matchmakers. I wonder if she was right."

"What was that?"

"She told me that perhaps if I wasn't quite so militantly against the idea, people might mind their own business."

"And what does that mean?"

Rachel sighed. "That I should just go along with it, I suppose."

"You mean, you'd have to date in order to avoid dating? That makes no sense at all. Where are we going?"

"Straight down Waukegan Street, eight blocks. Say that again?"

"What?"

"About dating. You're right. If I was seeing anybody at all, the well-meaning busybodies would smile and stay out of my life, wouldn't they?"

"Is that what I said?"

"And I wouldn't *really* have to be seeing anyone, as long as they all thought I was. That's what she meant, I'm sure of it."

"Don't you think the phantom lover would be a tough act to pull off?"

Rachel chewed on her bottom lip. "I suppose that's true. But if there was someone who understood..."

"You mean someone who's in the same boat, I suppose? Lady, if you're talking about me..."

Rachel blinked in surprise. "I wasn't. But now that you mention it..."

"I could be all sorts of terrible things, you know. A rapist, a serial killer..." He darted a glance at her. "I could even be a conservative, for all you know."

Rachel shook her head. "No. If you were anything so awful, your sisters-in-law wouldn't be trying to fix you up." She pointed. "It's that house there, the little one."

He pulled the car into the driveway and left the engine running while he looked at her thoughtfully for several seconds. "Your logic contains holes I could drive a truck through," he mused.

Embarrassment swept over her in a wave. How had she managed to make herself look like such a fruitcake?

She cleared her throat. "Absolutely. It's a silly idea. Forget it." She tried to push the car door open. It was heavy, and finally, anxious to escape, she gave it a shove with her foot. "Thanks for the ride."

As she ran for the tiny front porch, she heard the rumble of the car engine stop. She looked back to see him open the door and get out.

Now what? What was she going to do if he followed her? He could be any of the rotten things he had listed, or a whole lot more....

But he simply stood there as the rain poured down, with one elbow propped on the top of the car, the other on the door. Then he called, "You've got a point. It's the weirdest scheme I've ever heard, but it just might work. All right, we're dating. Saturday night all right with you?"

Rachel swallowed hard. "Sure. Why not?" she managed. "Um...excuse me. This is embarrassing, but...I can't remember your name."

Even in the rain she could see the sudden flash of his smile. "Let it be a challenge for you." And a moment later he was gone.

CHAPTER TWO

RACHEL FUMBLED with her key in the dim light of the front porch. On the other side of the door she could hear the strident protests of her Siamese cat.

"Bandit, at least let me get inside, all right?" she muttered. "I'm sorry I'm late, darling, but it's not my fault—it's the nasty rain."

The instant she stepped into the house, the shrieks settled into an uncompromisingly pitiful wail. In the dark, it took an instant for Rachel to locate where the sound was coming from; one irritated Siamese could sound like a chorus. But once her eyes adjusted, she spotted the streak of pale fawn fur balanced atop the couch in his Egyptian-statue pose, staring accusingly at her. But he unbent enough to allow her to scratch his neck.

"It's your own fault if you're hungry, Bandit," she said, letting her hand slide down the slick fur on his back. "I filled your dish this morning."

The cat raised his chin a little as if to say that dry cat meal did not, in his opinion, deserve to be called food. But when Rachel started for the kitchen he abandoned his haughty pose and swarmed down from the couch to follow.

She didn't even turn on the lights. The glow of a street lamp filtering through the gingham curtains let her see well enough to get a can from the cabinet. She scraped

Bandit's food into a bowl, poured herself a glass of grapefruit juice and leaned against the refrigerator door to contemplate the mess she'd just gotten herself into.

"What a way to solve a problem," she muttered. "Go out and create a whole new problem. Talk about jumping out of the frying pan and into the fire. Rachel Todd, you're an idiot."

How could she have behaved like such a fool? Getting herself involved, however tangentially, with a man she didn't even know.

It was temporary insanity, she told herself. She'd admit it. In fact, she would just call him up and tell him...

She gave a strangled groan. She could hardly call him up when she didn't remember his name.

It wasn't much comfort to tell herself that he might not remember hers, either—or at least not her first name. He had more information to work with than she did, and it would be no trick at all for him to find out what he didn't already know. Rachel, on the other hand, could hardly ask the women in the financial-aid office for the name of that handsome young pilot and then expect them not to be skeptical when she turned up on his arm just a day or two later.

Of course, she reflected, there was some comfort in knowing that not one of the coworkers would question her taste if they happened to spot her with him. That young man was awfully good-looking, and he had a smile to die for, not to mention a quick wit and the most expressive eyes she'd ever seen.

And what do you care? she asked herself rudely. It wasn't going to come to anything. And even if she intended to pursue her plot, how handsome he was had nothing to do with it. As long as he was presentable, the rest didn't matter.

She found herself wondering, however, exactly what he planned to do on Saturday night. What kind of entertainment would be to his taste? Movies? Concerts? Boxing?

She shivered at that last, then abruptly remembered Anne Garrett's dinner party. It had gone completely out of her mind earlier—along with any common sense she'd ever possessed, she thought crossly. Well, she'd simply tell her newfound friend that she had to go to a party. That would make it easier to get herself out of this mess, anyway....

Unless she took him along.

Don't be ridiculous, she told herself.

But, on the other hand, why shouldn't she? Anne had invited her to bring an escort, and if this young man hung around regularly with Nicolet's president and board of directors, he must have learned to be civilized in company. What better way to let the word get out that she wasn't against dating anymore? That was the whole point of the stupid scheme, after all.

She put her elbows on the counter and buried her head in her hands. She could hardly invite the man anywhere until she knew who he was.

RACHEL WASN'T EVEN INSIDE the financial-aid office the next morning before she started intercepting interested looks from her fellow workers. Or was it only her slightly guilty conscience that made her feel she was being stared at?

It's got to be your imagination, she told herself. None of them could possibly know anything about what had happened last night.

Her secretary greeted her with a knowing grin. "I let him put the stuff on your desk, Rachel, but I kept an eye on him just in case. He didn't touch a thing."

Rachel closed her eyes for a moment in pure pain. No wonder she'd gotten odd looks. What sort of "stuff" had he carried in, anyway?

And of course she couldn't come right out and ask her secretary just who it was who'd made this delivery!

She said stiffly, "Thank you, Amy," and swallowed hard before she opened the door of her office.

On her desk blotter lay a long-stemmed yellow rose, its petals still damp, and a new pocket-size collapsible umbrella. Rachel was just releasing a sigh of relief when she saw, half-hidden under the rose, a cream-colored card. A business card, she thought, and pounced on it.

But it was her own, apparently filched from the holder on the corner of her desk. So much for his not touching anything. Rachel wanted to swear.

On the back of it in deep blue ink, he'd written in tiny and precise letters: "Dearest Rachel, I hope you don't mind if I keep your other umbrella as a memento of a very special evening. Pink's not your color, anyway."

At that, she did swear. She'd forgotten all about the umbrella; she must have left it in his car. And as for her minding, did he seriously think she actually cared about that broken old thing?

Below the last line was an indecipherable scrawl. This was the signature—was it a short name or a set of initials—of the man who had so carefully written the note? Rachel could imagine the fiendish delight with which he'd done that. She turned the paper in all directions trying to make sense of it. Hmm. Could be an *A* and an *N*.

Anthony Newton, she thought wildly. No, that didn't sound familiar at all. Adam Nichols. Alex Novak. It was no comfort to know that sometime during that flight to Minneapolis, Ted Lehmann had told her the name of the pilot. She was certain of that much. The problem was, his name just hadn't been important enough to stick in her memory.

She picked up the telephone and dialed the president's office suite on the top floor of the administration building. Ted Lehmann's secretary sounded charming and unflappable. "How can I help you, Miss Todd?"

"I wondered how to get hold of the university's pilot."

"We don't have one. We always use Lakemont Aviation. Would you like the number?"

"A charter service?"

"Yes. We used to own a plane and have a pilot on staff, but it works better this way, because someone's always available. Just call the flying service at the airport, and they'll have a pilot get back to you."

"Wait," Rachel said desperately. "The man who flew Ted Lehmann to Minneapolis last week—who was he?"

"I don't remember, but it was probably Colin. He owns the business, and President Lehmann prefers to fly with him if he's available."

Rachel reached for the business card. If that's a capital *C*, she thought, I'm a monkey's uncle. Still... "And what's Colin's last name?"

"McKenna. But if it's Colin you need, I'm afraid you're out of luck. He left this morning to take President Lehmann to Chicago."

Colin McKenna, Rachel was thinking. Yes, "CM" was one possible interpretation of the scrawl. But the name still didn't sound familiar.

"Miss Todd? Is there anything else?"

"Oh . . . no. Thank you, you've been very helpful."

She phoned Lakemont Aviation and left a message for Colin McKenna. "Call Rachel Todd at Nicolet University," it said, and she gave the number that rang directly into her office. It was all she could do for the moment.

And if, when Colin McKenna called, he turned out to be the wrong pilot . . .

Well, Rachel thought, in that case I'll just have to make up a story about getting him mixed up with some student with a similar name, and I'll start over again.

Her head ached.

SHE MET DAWN MORGAN after work, and they spent an hour in the row of boutiques and gift shops across from the campus. "I'll give you a ride home," Dawn offered as they left the last store with their purchases. "I want to see where you're putting up these bookshelves, anyway."

When they got to the little house of Waukegan Street, there was already a car in the driveway. An old car. One Rachel had seen before. She studied it with trepidation.

But he's in Chicago, she thought.

She'd asked him to call, and he hadn't. Did that mean he'd simply come here, instead of telephoning, or was Colin McKenna the wrong person?

She turned to Dawn. "Would you mind if I didn't ask you in? I mean, some other time would be much better."

Dawn's eyebrows rose and she slanted a look at the car in the driveway. "I sense that something more entertaining has turned up," she said blandly. "Or perhaps I should say 'someone.'"

"It's not that. Really."

Just then there was a tap on the window beside Rachel. She rolled it down and stared into a pair of wide-set summer-blue eyes.

"Hi," he said huskily and leaned into the car. Very briefly his mouth brushed hers.

Rachel's stomach lurched all the way into her throat and lodged there. He pulled back and smiled a little, then peered in at Dawn. "Hello. Nice to meet you."

Dawn's eyes were as round as dinner plates. Rachel would have enjoyed the sight if she hadn't been so shaken.

"You're Crash McKenna," Dawn said.

The man outside the car winced a little. "I've been called that, yes. I prefer Colin." Rachel smothered a sigh of relief.

"And you're Dawn...Morgan, right?" he said, opening Rachel's door and holding out a hand to assist her. "Thank you for bringing Rachel home."

Rachel automatically began to protest the proprietary tone. She swallowed the rest of her sentence, however, as the grip on her wrist tightened to almost crushing force.

"Anytime," Dawn said. "I'll see you tomorrow, Rachel."

And she'll want the full story, too, Rachel thought with a groan. At least she'd have a chance to think it over first; she owed Colin thanks for that much. Still, he had been unnecessarily high-handed about it.

Colin took the shopping bags from her hand. "What did you do, relieve the stores of all their inventory? These weigh a ton."

"Is what I buy your business?" Rachel fumbled for her key. "Just when I was beginning to consider the advantages of your being out of town," she said acidly, "you turn up."

"I tried to call. You'd already left your office by the time I was finished at the airport. It took you longer than I expected to catch up with me," he mused. "The answering service said that your message didn't come in till after ten o'clock this morning."

"You could have told me you owned the business. Even when I got a name, I wasn't sure it was you." Rachel pushed the front door open. She'd left the television on that morning, and tonight Bandit was less agitated. He roused from a nap on the cushion of her favorite rocking chair, yawned, stretched and then stared unblinkingly at her visitor.

"That would have taken all the fun out of it, don't you think?"

Rachel hung their coats in the tiny entry closet. When she turned back to face him, Colin was standing in the middle of the room, inspecting the place.

The house was tiny, but it was the perfect size for her—just a living room, small bedroom at the back, with kitchen and bath in between. She had arranged her furniture at angles to create an inviting little nook by the fireplace, and she had hung a few pictures on the walls. Her new bookshelves were stacked in a corner, sanded smooth and ready to install. Once they were in place on the short wall between the mantel and the window, she could unpack the boxes of books and knickknacks, and the little house would truly be home.

Colin turned around. In his arms lay the cat. Bandit's blue eyes, almost precisely the same color as Colin's, were half-closed, and he wore an expression of utter contentment. In fact, he looked so indecently relaxed he could have been boneless.

Rachel was astounded, for she'd never seen her cat take to a stranger so easily before. What was there about this man that seemed to automatically lower defenses?

"I think we'd better talk," she said. "Would you like a cup of coffee?"

Colin followed her into the kitchen. Bandit swarmed out of his arms onto the counter and demanded his supper. Rachel put the cat and his bowl on the floor and started the coffeepot. Then she sat down at the tiny table. Colin hadn't said a word.

His silence annoyed her, and she heard herself asking, "Does Ted Lehmann know your nickname is Crash?"

"I doubt it. And just to clear up any misgivings you may have, I've never damaged an airplane."

She looked at him doubtfully. "Then how did you get the name? And who gave it to you?"

"It was all because of my first perfect three-point landing."

"Wait a minute. I thought you said it didn't have anything to do with an airplane."

"That was the problem," Colin explained patiently. "I wasn't flying a plane at that particular moment. I was driving the family car and imagining the best of all possible landings. You've heard of creative visualization, where you picture yourself doing something well, so the next time you actually do it your performance improves?"

Rachel nodded. "I've heard of it. I'm just not sure I want to hear what happened when you tried it."

"At the very moment in my visualization when the plane touched the ground, I did precisely what I was supposed to do, except of course the steering wheel didn't respond like the controls of a plane. I hit the tree at the end of the driveway."

"How old were you?"

"Seventeen, I think."

Rachel stared at him. "And your parents let you fly after that?"

"Of course. They just didn't let me drive. My brothers didn't stop calling me Crash until I outgrew them all and could make my threats stick." He propped his elbows on the table and said warmly, "This is a great idea, Rachel—getting to know each other. Now tell me about you. Do you have an interesting nickname?"

She shook her head. "Getting to know each other wasn't exactly what I had in mind."

"Oh. Then what?"

"Colin, I don't like the way this is going. Let's just cancel the whole thing, all right?"

The coffeepot gave a final asthmatic sigh. Colin got up. "Cups?" he asked.

"In the cabinet above the pot."

He poured the coffee and brought her cup over. "What about your friend in the car tonight? We had her convinced."

Rachel sighed. "If I'm lucky, she'll think she was hallucinating."

"But it's going to be really easy. No woman in her right mind would ever dream of a hoax like this."

"Thanks," Rachel said coolly.

Colin grinned. "I didn't mean you. Look, have you eaten? Let's discuss this over dinner. How about the little Chinese place down by the campus?"

"I don't think we should be seen together in public. It will just create more questions like the ones Dawn will be asking tomorrow, and if we're not going to go on with this..."

"All right, be a quitter, but it all still makes sense to me. Besides, there has to have been a reason you thought it up in the first place. I mean, if you're so happy with things the way they are, this whole scheme would never have occurred to you."

Rachel tried to ignore the comment, but the gentle inquisitiveness in his eyes didn't go away. Finally she said, "The Fall Festival. Everyone seems to be determined I have a date for it, no matter what lengths they have to go to."

Colin shrugged. "So now you've got one. What's there to lose? You said yourself I'm an upstanding citizen. Besides, you owe me one."

Rachel shook her head in confusion. "One what?"

"One person of my choice convinced I've got no need for help in the dating department. I took care of your friend Dawn, so you owe—"

"You mean your sister-in-law, I suppose?"

Colin grinned. "Bingo. Then we'll be square."

Rachel considered. "She'd be a lot tougher than Dawn was."

"Very true. That's why I think we might just as well proceed with the original plan."

Rachel sipped her coffee. "And I suppose if I don't cooperate, you'll tell Dawn the whole thing's a sham? Well, it wasn't my idea to convince her we're practically lovers, so..."

He considered that for a moment and shook his head. "No. I wouldn't. Upstanding citizens don't descend to blackmail, Rachel. But why are you getting cold feet, anyway? It was your idea in the first place, and nothing's changed, has it? Unless you do something, all the same people are still going to be trying to fix you up for the festival.''

It was an excellent question, so why was she feeling jittery? It wasn't as if she was really getting involved with him. And if Dawn's reaction was any indication... Colin had a point. It would be as easy as he said, because who would suspect them of faking?

"You're right," she said suddenly.

"I don't know why you sound surprised. Is it a deal?" He held out his hand, and Rachel shook it.

"Through Fall Festival," she said.

"That's only two weeks away. I think my sister-in-law will need a little longer than that to be convinced."

"Like how long?" Rachel said doubtfully.

"How about Thanksgiving?"

"That's six weeks!"

"It's not a life sentence, Rachel. Actually, keeping the scheme up till Christmas might be better."

"Christmas?" Her voice was shrill. "You must be joking."

"No? Well, I suppose I can explain that you're going out of town to visit your family or something."

Rachel chewed her bottom lip. "All right," she said finally. "Thanksgiving it is."

"That'll do. If I play it right, I should be free of interference till spring at least." He sounded quite pleased about the idea. "Now let's go get some food. And Saturday night we can start with—"

"A dinner party for which I need an escort."

Colin frowned. "Dinner party?"

"What did *you* have in mind? Sorry, but I forgot that I've already committed myself for the evening." Rachel wrinkled her nose a little. "Perhaps it's not your kind of thing," she admitted. "It's being given by one of Nicolet's big donors. If you'd rather not go, Colin..."

He sighed and rubbed the back of his neck as if he were in pain. "I'll go," he said. "I've already turned down an incredible invitation for Saturday night because I had a date with you, so I may as well be a sport about your dinner party." Then he grinned. "Who knows? Some of these stuffed shirts turn out to be fun when you poke them hard enough."

No, Rachel told herself. He wouldn't dare.

They grabbed their coats and went out to his car. She half expected the broken umbrella to still be on the floor. When she didn't see it, she asked what he'd done with it. "Buried it ceremoniously in a trash Dumpster, I hope," she added. "The thing was useless."

Colin looked shocked. "You wouldn't expect me to admit it to you if I threw it away."

"Yes, I would."

"But it's a sentimental souvenir."

"There's no need to pretend that this arrangement of ours is anything it isn't, at least not when we're alone."

Colin started the engine, then turned to study her for a moment. "Meaning what?"

"Meaning we tell the truth, instead of pussyfooting about with sociable white lies. For instance, I am not going to hesitate to tell you that I absolutely refuse to eat Chinese food. I hate the stuff."

"It's my very favorite," he said mournfully.

Rachel shrugged. "You've got a right. Still, that's no reason to martyr myself over it."

"I bet if this was a real date you'd eat Chinese and smile."

"Possibly," Rachel conceded. "That's one of the reasons I'm glad it's not a real date."

Colin grinned. "What else do you want to tell me?"

Rachel shook her head. "I didn't say I was going to bare my soul, just that I don't plan to get hung up in social lies in an effort to impress you. How about Mexican?"

"Too spicy. Do you like seafood?"

"That's fine. See? There are always compromises."

"Is that why you have such a stunning success rate with your dates? Your willingness to compromise?"

"You don't need to be sarcastic, Colin. If I choose not to date, it's certainly no one's business but mine."

She thought, as they drove, that he had gone permanently silent. But as they got out of the car at the restaurant, he confided, "That's what puzzles me, you see. If you were just complaining about the caliber of men your friends were fixing you up with, I could understand. But to refuse to have anything to do with men at all..."

"Let it be a challenge to you," Rachel said crisply.

He obviously recognized the quotation, for his eyes lighted with an appreciative sparkle.

"Besides, you're in the same boat," she added.

"Oh, no," Colin said earnestly. "I never said I didn't want to date. But I'm the only unmarried member of my family now, and I've had no peace since the last wedding."

A smiling waiter showed them to a table in a quiet corner, perfect for intimate conversations and holding hands. Rachel decided to take this as a good sign; if waiters believed they were a twosome, fooling the rest of the world should be no problem at all.

"How many sisters-in-law did you say you have?" Rachel asked as she glanced at the menu.

"Three. Fortunately only one of them lives here in Lakemont."

"That's the one you were complaining about last night?"

Colin nodded. "But the other two are coming to visit for Thanksgiving. It's one of the big holidays in my family, you see, and they'll all be clucking about poor lonely Colin turning thirty and getting set in his ways."

"Can't you just tell them to mind their own business?"

"Certainly I can. In fact, I frequently have, with the same marvelous results as when you tell your friends not to butt into your life."

"Point well made." Rachel closed the menu. "I think I'll have the lobster. Would you rather take turns picking up the bill when we eat out, or have separate checks each time?"

Colin didn't even blink. "Oh, let's take turns. Separate checks are so tacky. Not to mention being a dead giveaway if anyone happens to be watching."

The vigilant waiter bustled over with their drinks, and Colin ordered Rachel's lobster and a salmon steak with dill sauce for himself.

As soon as the waiter was gone, Rachel said, "You did that so smoothly I hardly realized I'd been preempted."

"You're not going to go all feminist on me, are you? It's pure habit. My father always orders for my mother, you see."

"They must be sticklers for manners." That didn't quite fit with the image she had formed earlier. Would parents like that let a teenager take flying lessons?

"Oh, it isn't a matter of etiquette, really. Mother's a lovely woman, but she's a little vague about details sometimes. It drives my father crazy when she can't make up her mind what to eat, so he took over the job long ago." He shrugged. "Actually I think she'd live happily on bread and cheese and never notice what she was missing." He picked up his glass. "To the grand new scheme of things."

Rachel raised her stemmed goblet and cast a curious look at his Perrier water. "Does it bother you that I have a glass of wine?"

One dark eyebrow quirked a little. "If it did, would you send it back?"

"No. But I wouldn't ever order another one when I was with you."

He smiled a little. "Be careful, Rachel, you're beginning to sound as if you're trying to please me."

"Not a chance."

"Well, don't worry about it. There are definite rules about the time required between drinking alcohol and flying, but I decided a long time ago that the two things don't mix at all, and since I never know when I'll be flying, I just don't drink. But I'm not rabid on the subject of other people's consumption."

"What do you mean, you never know when you'll be flying? Are you always on call?"

"Most of the time. Our clients are unpredictable. And of course we have an emergency run now and then for the university hospital."

"You mean transplants and things?"

Colin nodded. "Since most of the guys who work for me have families, I'm usually the one who goes. But don't feel too sorry for me—I'm the one who schedules it that way. I'd spend twenty hours a day in the air if the regulations would let me."

She leaned back in her chair. "When did you first know you wanted to fly?"

Colin shrugged. "Beats me. I don't remember a time I didn't want to. My father says he knew the day I got my very first helium balloon and lost my grip on the string. I didn't scream about it like most toddlers do, he said. I just stood there and watched with this very odd look in my eyes as it soared into the sky."

Rachel smiled. "And when you discovered birds, I suppose you started jumping out of trees and flapping your arms."

"Something like that. Then there was my first flight ever. I'd saved my allowance for months so I could have fifteen minutes in a single-engine plane circling over Lakemont. Most people were looking for their houses. I was inspecting the equipment."

Rachel's lobster was good, but it got only half her attention; the other half was on Colin's stock of amusing stories. Whenever he stopped, she prompted him on. When the waiter brought the bill, Rachel glanced at her wristwatch in surprise. She was astounded to realize how much of the evening had gone while they talked.

Rachel rummaged for her credit card, but Colin shook his head. "Ladies do not always go first," he said, reaching for his wallet.

"But my lobster was most of the bill."

"If you're planning to keep track of things like that, Rachel, you're going to be a very dull girl." He smiled at the waiter and told him to keep the change, then came around the table to pull out her chair.

"Well...thank you. I'll pay next time."

"Maybe I'll hold out for Lakemont Grande," he said. "Best steaks in town."

"I haven't been there."

"Then we'll definitely go. A week from Saturday, perhaps?"

Rachel said coolly, "Why don't we see how this weekend goes first?"

As Colin walked her to her door, he mused, "I've been thinking it wouldn't hurt if we practiced a few things."

Rachel found her key and inserted it in the lock. "Have you got something particular in mind?" she asked warily.

"Oh, just things like good-night kisses."

"What?" Her voice was practically a shriek.

"Only so we don't look like amateurs, you understand," he added earnestly.

"We're not going to be putting on shows!"

"I agree, of course, that sex shouldn't be a spectator sport. Buy my whole family tends to be the openly affectionate sort, so if we're going to satisfy them we're serious..."

"You did very well at convincing Dawn without rehearsals."

"Thank you, Rachel." He gave a formal little bow. "I'm honored by your high opinion. You have a great deal of experience, I assume? Still, that was just an ordinary garden-variety kiss, and—"

"That's the only kind you're likely to get around here, Colin." She twisted the key and turned to face him. "Thank you for dinner and a lovely evening."

He tugged lightly on the lobe of her ear. "You're a fraud, Rachel."

She blinked in surprise. "What do you mean?"

"You said you weren't going to tell white lies for the sake of impressing me," he reminded her, and drew his finger slowly down her face, across her cheekbone and the curve of her jaw. "See you Saturday."

CHAPTER THREE

WHEN THE DOORBELL RANG for the fifth time that day, Rachel happened to be juggling a carpenter's level, a drill and the metal rod that would form half the support for her bookshelves. She swore with surprising distinctness, considering the pencil she had gripped between her teeth, and decided to ignore the bell. After all, on three of the previous four occasions her callers had been neighborhood kids selling candy to raise funds for their school. The fourth visitor had been Dawn Morgan in an inquisitive mood—which had been enough to give Rachel fond thoughts of the youthful salesfolk.

So she adjusted the rod another fraction of an inch until it was absolutely vertical, managed to lay the level aside without losing her grip on the rod and balanced the drill to start a pilot hole for the first screw.

The bell rang again.

Rachel glanced over her shoulder at the shadow on the glass panel in the door. The silhouette was too big to be another budding entrepreneur, and too broad-shouldered to be Dawn or any of her other female friends.

"And too stubborn for his own good," she muttered. She put the tools down and answered the door. "It's Saturday afternoon," she pointed out. "The dinner party does not begin for another six hours. In the meantime—"

"You've started to get ready?" Colin asked brightly. "The new hair color is interesting, but I liked it better plain red."

Rachel's fingertips went to her hair and encountered gritty dust from the few holes she'd already managed to drill in the plaster. She must look like a graying grandma.

"My hair is not red," she corrected automatically.

"My mistake. Actually I stopped by because you didn't tell me what time the party is, or the location, or what to wear."

Rachel sighed. "Seven o'clock, twelve Pemberton Place Lane, and it's black tie—which, come to think of it, I suppose you don't have." She ran her fingers through her tangle of auburn curls and looked up at him, her hazel eyes anxious. "Well, you'll just have to find a tux somewhere, because I've already told the hostess I'm bringing an escort, so you can't back out now." She picked up her tools and started in again, trying to get the support rod lined up just right.

"Nice of you to give me plenty of notice."

Rachel knew she shouldn't be annoyed at the remark; after all, he was right. "Do I have to think of everything?" she muttered.

"Apparently so." Colin moved over beside her, took the pencil out of her mouth and marked the spot on the wall where she was holding the rod.

"Thanks." She put the level aside and picked up the drill. "You can bring me the bill for the tuxedo rental."

"That's thoughtful of you. Want me to put up that rod?"

"I can manage. I got the first one up just fine, didn't I?"

He didn't answer. Rachel stole a glance at him and decided he looked as if he had his doubts. Did he think she was fool enough not to make sure the shelves were securely anchored?

"Have a candy bar," she said. "I bought three of them this morning. Or if you'd rather have coffee, you know where everything is."

He did not disappear into the kitchen as she'd hoped. Instead, he pulled a chair around, propped one arm on the back of it and ate a candy bar while he watched.

Rachel finished installing the rod and tested it, then opened a box of brackets and began tapping them into place with her hammer to support the wooden shelves.

Colin crumpled the empty wrapper and aimed it at the nearest wastebasket. "Who taught you to do things like this?"

Rachel shrugged. "When you need something and there's no one around to lean on, you just learn." She dusted off her hands and picked up a shelf board from the pile. The wall was short, the shelf light, and she slid it easily into place. "Dawn was here earlier today. Full of questions, I might add. One of her teaching assistants saw us at the restaurant and happened to mention to her how cozy we looked."

"Cozy?"

"That was Dawn's word. I have no idea how the woman formed that opinion."

Colin shrugged. "Spies always turn up where you least expect them."

Rachel frowned. "It was a good thing you paid the bill, I suppose. Why is it that society still frowns on women paying for things, anyway? It's perfectly normal."

Colin didn't comment on that. He looked her over thoughtfully and said at last, "Rachel, what do you have against men?"

The question caught her off guard. "Nothing. I—"

"Or is it one particular man who gave you this hang-up? You act like a woman who's been badly hurt. I'm just not sure how."

She picked up the next shelf and took her time putting it into place. With her back still toward him, she said, "I don't know what you mean."

"That's baloney. You just don't want to talk about it. What terrible thing did he do, anyway? Force you to eat Chinese food?"

Relieved by the abrupt shift of mood, Rachel laughed. "Something like that."

Colin didn't crack a smile. "Now we're getting somewhere. At least you're admitting there was a man."

Rachel's stomach felt wobbly. Had she admitted that?

"You said something about having no one to lean on. What did you mean?"

"Please, Colin, it's not important, all right?"

He stayed obstinately silent.

Rachel sighed. "I just meant I don't have any family. My parents divorced when I was little, and my mother died a few years ago. You may complain about family interference, but from my point of view it sounds rather wonderful to have a bunch of brothers."

Colin didn't answer right away, and she held her breath, waiting for the next question. But when he did speak, Rachel relaxed, for he'd let the subject drop.

"You'll get over that delusion in a hurry, I expect, once you see what it's really like. Which reminds me, there's a family dinner tomorrow at my parents' house."

Rachel almost dropped a shelf. "All the family?"

"Oh, no, just the local branches. It's sort of a Sunday tradition."

She slid the shelf onto the brackets and pulled a small ladder into place so she could put the top one up. "Colin," she began cautiously, "is it really necessary to go to these lengths? We don't have to go everywhere together, surely. I don't object to putting on a show for your family—I know it's part of the deal—but I was thinking more in terms of a once-a-week date."

"Were you? Personally, I think it would be a good idea to be seen together a lot right at first. You know, get the word out quickly and stop the plotters in their tracks. Then we can safely slack off a bit."

Rachel bit her lip. She supposed he did have a point.

"Tomorrow, twelve o'clock," Colin went on. "And it would be even better if we went to church together first."

Rachel glared at him. "You have got to be kidding."

"You don't generally go to services?"

"It's not that. I'd be afraid of being struck down by lightning if I used the church to flesh out a trick like this. It would be like telling lies under oath."

"All right. No church. You will come to dinner, though?"

Rachel looked doubtful. "Are you sure it wouldn't be better if you broke the news by yourself tomorrow, so it wouldn't come as a shock when I walk in? There's plenty of time before Thanksgiving, you know."

Colin shook his head. "For one thing, it won't be a shock. Don't forget Patrick saw you at the ice-cream shop, so the word's already out, believe me. For another thing, if you don't promise to come tomorrow, I'll have second thoughts about tonight. It's not too late for me to go bowling with the guys."

"Bowling? So that was the incredible invitation you turned down to have a date with me."

Colin shrugged. "It beats staying home alone. And it also beats dressing up like a penguin for a dull dinner party. So if you don't feel up to acting the part tomorrow..."

"You said you didn't believe in blackmail," Rachel reminded him.

Colin smiled. "That was before I got to know you better, darling. Shall I go round up a tux or not?"

"Sunday dinner with the family," she said meekly. "What a wonderful idea. How thoughtful of you to include me. I'd be honored."

He tapped the tip of her nose with a gentle fingertip. "Don't lay it on too thick, Rachel, dear," he warned, "or your nose is apt to start growing like Pinocchio's, and then even my mother might notice something amiss."

RACHEL SPENT most of the rest of the afternoon unpacking boxes of books. But she was ready half an hour early, and she found herself pacing the tiny living room, listening to the rhythmic click of her heels against the hardwood floor and feeling the flutter of nervousness in the pit of her stomach.

Nerves! She was as much on edge as if this was a real first date. She scolded herself for the foolish reaction and sat down with a magazine, determined to relax.

Of course, she honestly did have something to be nervous about. Colin might not have found a tux on such short notice. And if he hadn't—

The doorbell rang, and she tossed the magazine aside and rushed to answer it. When she flung open the door she released a little sigh of relief. His black tuxedo was faultless, and it fit like a dream. There was a gleam of unholy amusement in his eyes, but suddenly it faded as he looked at her. She felt cool dread creeping over her.

"What's wrong?" Her hand touched the gold nugget at her throat, then slid down her black velvet cocktail dress, skimming the row of tiny pearl buttons that marched down the front below the heart-shaped neckline. Her fingertips came to rest at the nipped-in waistline. The velvet felt sensually soft against her fingertips. What could he be objecting to? She was certainly dressed properly for a party of this sort. That was what she liked about velvet; it was elegant and sophisticated, and always in style.

Colin's gaze had followed the hesitant motion of her hand, then moved on to the hemline of the narrow skirt and paused as if he couldn't quite believe what he was seeing.

"Do you think my skirt's too short?" Rachel shifted her feet nervously.

He swallowed hard. "Not with legs like those. Where's your coat?"

She picked up a fur jacket that had been draped over the back of a chair and handed it to him. As she turned away to let him help her, Colin gave a strangled gasp. "There's no back in that thing!"

Rachel looked over her shoulder. "There certainly is. It just happens to be lace, that's all."

"Black lace, with no lining. Are you wearing a bra?"

"What kind of question is that, Colin?"

He swallowed hard. "A stupid one. Obviously you're not. Well, it will take everyone's mind off the length of your skirt, that's for sure."

"Just help me put my coat on."

"Yes, ma'am." His tone was not nearly as subservient as his words. He placed the fur jacket carefully around her, letting his fingers sink into the softness at her shoulders. "Nice little thing," he said. "What sort of beast used to wear it?"

"Thousands of poor little polyesters gave their lives for this coat."

"It's fake?" He bent to rub his nose against the collar, and Rachel jerked her head aside. "Wow," Colin said thoughtfully. "It's a hell of a good fake, I'll say that for it. You smell wonderful, by the way. What's the perfume?"

She was darned if she was going to tell him she was wearing Midnight Passion. Why did cosmetic companies have to give such suggestive names to scents, anyway? She stepped away from him and picked up her tiny handbag. "I thought we'd take my car tonight," she said tentatively.

The humor was back in his eyes. "What's the matter? You don't think mine fits with the staid, old-money image of Pemberton Place? I'll have you know it's a great car. The only reason I haven't traded it in for a new one is that it's going to be a classic."

"Any day now, I'd say."

But as soon as they were in the garage, Rachel realized that Colin didn't seem to fit too well with her car. He eyed the little blue convertible with trepidation, ran a hand across the top and muttered under his breath as he tried to fit himself comfortably behind the wheel. "A convertible in Wisconsin? What are you thinking of? We get enough snow up here to cave the roof in."

Rachel snuggled the soft collar of her coat up around her face. The car had been in the garage all day. Now she wished she'd pulled it out into the sunshine; at least that way the leather seats wouldn't have been quite so frigid. "I admit it doesn't make a lot of sense in this climate, but in Arizona it was great."

"Is that where you came from? The land of heatstroke and Gila monsters?" He slid the driver's seat back as far as it would go. "I've got it. You didn't buy a convertible because it's a status symbol. You bought it because with a car this size anybody taller than a yardstick can't get in unless he puts the top down and uses a crowbar. Right?"

"Colin, did I ever warn you that I get homicidal over jokes about short people?"

He looked astounded. "But Rachel, light of my life, I wasn't talking about you. I never would have implied that you are anything but perfect!"

She sniffed. "Just how old were you when you kissed the Blarney stone?"

"Fourteen."

"I knew it."

"Now you'll never believe anything I say, will you?"

He sounded almost sad, but Rachel didn't think he meant it for an instant.

"It wasn't my idea to go to Blarney Castle, anyway," he explained. "It was Dad's sabbatical, and he took the whole family to Ireland. Believe me, after the years he'd spent saving for that trip, anyone who hadn't participated fully would not have lived to come home, so when it was time for Blarney—"

"Sabbatical? Does he teach?"

"Math to undergrads here at Nicolet. He seems to like impossible causes. He even tried to instill a love of calculus in all five of us kids."

The car slowed to a sedate pace and eased over the speed bump at the entrance to Pemberton Place. Once the most expensive neighborhood in Lakemont, it was still among the most exclusive; even the streets were owned and maintained by the residents, rather than the city, and at night the gates were closed. Rachel was surprised there wasn't a security man at the entrance around the clock just to keep out casual tourists.

"There are five of you?" Rachel asked. "I thought you said you had three sisters-in-law."

Colin nodded. "That's right. Dad met with varying success with his indoctrination in math, I might add. He got an accountant and a banker out of us, but then there's the real-estate tycoon and me." He stopped.

"That's four," Rachel prompted. "What about the other one?"

He turned the car into a circular drive and brought it to a smooth halt in front of a Tudor-revival mansion built of paving brick and carved stone. Light from the leaded casement windows spilled down the front steps.

"Oh, you probably know her," he said easily. "She's done rather well for herself—she married the Lakemont *Chronicle*. Her name's Anne Garrett."

Rachel closed her eyes in pain.

Colin came around to open her door and help her out.

Rachel would have liked to clutch his arm to keep her wobbly knees under control, but that would have let him know how thoroughly shaken she was, and she suspected he was enjoying her reaction quite enough as it was.

"This isn't one of Anne's larger parties, I see," Colin mused. "There's no valet to park the cars."

Rachel couldn't stop herself any longer. "Dammit, Colin, you could have told me Anne Garrett's your sister!"

"I assumed Anne had told you."

"I never talked to her," Rachel hissed. "I just left a message that I was bringing a guest. I didn't even give your name."

"In that case," Colin said thoughtfully, pressing the doorbell, "this could really be fun."

The double front doors opened before them, and it was too late to argue about it, because the butler was bowing a greeting. "Good evening, Miss Todd," he said. "Hello, Mr. McKenna."

Rachel stepped across the threshold into a huge foyer. It was at least sixteen feet to the carved plaster ceiling. Under her feet was the subdued sheen of an old Persian carpet, and against the walnut-paneled walls gleamed several exquisite oil paintings.

Colin seemed to pay no attention to the surroundings. But of course, Rachel thought, he must be used to them.

He tenderly removed her jacket and handed it to the white-haired butler. "Very good, Thomas," he applauded. "Not even a hint of surprise. Do you think my sister will be pleased to see me?"

The butler allowed himself a half smile. "'Shocked' is probably more like it." He raised his voice a little. "Mr. and Mrs. Garrett are in the drawing room." He indicated an arched doorway to the left of the foyer.

As if she'd heard the butler, Anne Garrett appeared in the open archway, hands braced against the walnut paneling. "Rachel!" she said eagerly. "Do come in. I want you to meet my husband. And this must be your—" She stopped, shook her head, cleared her throat and finished flatly, "—guest."

Beside her, Rachel could feel Colin's body quivering. With amusement, she guessed.

"Hello, Colin," Anne said.

He stepped forward and brushed her cheek with his lips. "Hello, Annie," he said gently.

For one long moment Anne Garrett said nothing, merely looked at him. Then she laughed, a low musical sound, and shook her head. "You're a devil, Colin. Now come in before the rest of the guests get so curious they come out to see what's going on." She swept them into the spacious drawing room.

Rachel recognized most of the guests' names, though several she had never met. Intercepting a speculative look from a bright-eyed little woman who was introduced as the wife of Nicolet's president, she remembered Anne's warning about Dorie Lehmann's inclination toward matchmaking. Her fingers tightened a little on Colin's sleeve.

Ted Lehmann came toward her, his warm voice booming, and drew her, with Colin following, across the room to a gray-haired man standing in front of the fireplace. "Jim, this is Rachel Todd, the miracle worker I've been telling you about. She's been on the staff at Nicolet four months now, and she's already hit a new vein of donations. Rachel, this is Jim Garrett, who's on our board of directors."

Rachel put out a hand. Jim Garrett was tall and straight and still handsome, but even his stunning smile could not conceal the years written in the lines on his face. The man must be twice Anne's age, she thought.

Anne's done rather well for herself, Colin had said just a few minutes ago. *She married the Lakemont Chronicle . . .* It looked as if he'd been telling the simple truth.

Don't jump to conclusions, Rachel reminded herself. It's certainly none of your business. Perhaps Anne really loves him.

"Thank you for inviting me, Mr. Garrett," she murmured. "You have a lovely home."

He laughed. "Not mine anymore, I'm glad to say. Anne and Matt think I made them a very generous wedding gift, so don't tell them I was delighted to pass the headache on to the younger generation, all right?" He winked at someone behind her.

"I heard that," Anne said. "And I don't believe a word of it—except for it being a generous gift. Rachel, meet my husband, Matt."

This is more like it, Rachel thought. The man beside Anne was in his mid-thirties, tall and rangy, with hair the color of honey and a smile every bit as striking as his father's.

He took Rachel's hand. "It's always nice to meet a miracle worker, Miss Todd."

Rachel lowered her gaze. She wished Ted Lehmann hadn't said that.

"How about telling us what it is you've done to earn that title?" Matt said. "It sounds intriguing."

"Oh, I—"

"She'll pass it off as nothing," Ted interrupted. "So I'll tell you, Matt. Rachel has taken a special interest in students who don't quite fit the profile for financial aid, but who would have to leave Nicolet without it. And she's miraculously managed to match them up with funds so they can stay in school."

Colin looked puzzled. "But isn't that what you're supposed to do?" he asked.

"Exactly," Rachel said. "And it's not as if these are endowed scholarships, either. They're special grants for these few students. It's no big deal, really."

"See?" Ted said. "She's belittling herself again. What she didn't say is that there are ten of these students now,

and their tuition is being paid with entirely new money—
funds Nicolet would never have seen if it weren't for
Rachel's connections. She saw these students were in
need, so she went after the money to help them and she
got it." He said, obviously savoring the sound of it,
"They're being sponsored by the Carleton Fund." He
paused and darted a look at Rachel, then added quickly,
"At any rate, it's the sort of thing that's earned her the
title of miracle worker."

Matt Garrett whistled. "That's not peanuts. How did
you find this fund, anyway?"

Rachel said coolly, "Every financial-aid officer in the
country has a few special resources—people to call on
when nothing else works."

"That's no answer," Colin muttered.

She gave him a level look. "It wasn't intended to be an
answer. If I were to tell where I found Carleton, every
financial-aid officer worth his salt would know where to
look. And Carleton wouldn't like that at all. So I'm sure
we can all agree to let the subject drop."

"Hear, hear," Dorie Lehmann chimed in. "That's
enough about business for one evening, anyway, Ted. I
thought you promised me that for a few hours we could
all let Nicolet take care of itself. Rachel, come sit beside
me." She patted the love-seat cushion.

Thank heaven, Rachel thought, she'd come with a
date. If Anne had been right about Dorie Lehmann's
propensity for matchmaking, Colin's presence would
spare her. Dorie smiled warmly at her and said, "Do tell
me about that lovely necklace you've been fiddling
with."

Rachel looked down in surprise to find her fingers
clasped about the gold nugget she wore. She hadn't realized she'd been nervously toying with it, but perhaps

if she was lucky no one had recognized it as a sign of uneasiness.

"So unusual," Dorie murmured.

"You were prospecting in Arizona and found it," Colin speculated. He was still standing nearby.

"Sorry to disappoint you. It *is* one of a kind, but not quite that unusual. It's made from my family's rings and odd bits of jewelry. The jeweler salvaged all the gold and melted it down, then poured it into water and let it cool into a free-form nugget. Then he took the stones that had been in the rings and set them here and there in the crevices."

"What a magnificent idea," Anne said, leaning over the back of the love seat to get a better look. She laughed. "Of course, any of the McKennas who ever had a bit of jewelry worth salvaging is still wearing it."

That was certainly true of the diamond that flashed on Anne's left hand, Rachel thought, and of the double strand of pearls at her throat.

"These things weren't much in their original state," Rachel said quickly. "I'd never have melted down really good things. Some of the bands were worn thin, and most of the stones were no more than chips. But I think it's rather pretty now."

"It's lovely," Dorie said warmly. "And much more practical than putting the things away in your jewelry box. You're obviously a down-to-earth young woman."

"Yes, isn't she?" Anne murmured. "Ah, here's Thomas to announce dinner."

Rachel found herself seated between Jim Garrett and Ted Lehmann, who unfolded his napkin and said, "I'm sorry if I embarrassed you, Rachel. Dorie gave me a good scolding over it."

Rachel's eyes widened. "She did?" she asked baldly. "I was sitting beside her, and she didn't say a word to you before dinner."

Ted smiled. "Believe me, when you've been married for thirty years you don't need words to know when you're in trouble. I know perfectly well the Carleton Fund business is confidential, and even though this group is rock-solid safe, it was thoughtless of me to get carried away with pride and announce it. It won't happen again."

"Thank you," Rachel said. "I appreciate that."

Jim Garrett poked at his appetizer and said, "How did you get into financial aid, Rachel? It seems a strange place for you."

She nodded. "It's not exactly the kind of thing kids say they want to be when they grow up, is it? Well, it wasn't my first choice, either."

Across the table Colin looked up from the trout mousse on his plate. His gaze was intent.

"But I needed all the help I could get to make it through college. In fact, I worked in the financial-aid office while I was a student, so I saw all aspects of what the counselors did, and I appreciated the effort they made to keep me in school. After I graduated, there was a position open, so I took it." She shrugged. "I've been working my way up the ladder ever since."

"Always in Arizona?" Jim Garrett asked. "This climate must be a real switch for you."

Rachel wet her lips. "No. I grew up in Michigan actually. I'd only been in Arizona a few years."

"Didn't Anne tell me you've got a degree in accounting?"

"Yes. And when I've settled in a little more, I'm going to start on my doctorate in academic administration."

"I think she's after my job," Ted said. He sounded uneasy, but Rachel saw the twinkle in his eyes.

"Don't worry," she murmured. "It'll take me years to finish. You'll be happily retired by the time I'm ready to move in."

He clapped his hand to his chest and gave an exaggerated sigh of relief. "Thank heaven. Then I can just carry on with business as usual. Colin, did my secretary get in touch with you? We've got a young man coming in next weekend, and he'll need shuttle service from Chicago."

Colin shook his head. "I haven't gotten a message."

"If you've made plans, one of the other pilots will do. At least it's a Sunday, though. I hate asking you to give up your Saturday nights."

Colin smiled. "Because it might interfere with my love life?"

At that precise instant, the whole table went silent, and though Colin's voice was pitched at a conversational level, he might as well have been shouting. And of course he'd been looking thoughtfully at Rachel as he spoke, and now everyone was studying her.

She looked down at her plate. The butler had just removed her appetizer and replaced it with a delicate arrangement of sliced roast duck and sautéed vegetables. All of a sudden she wasn't very hungry.

Still nobody said anything. From the corner of her eye she could see Anne's face. She looked as if she'd choked on the last bit of her trout mousse.

"Don't fret, Ted," Colin went on gently. "I won't miss out on anything, because I'll just take the light of my life along with me. In fact, we might go to Chicago Saturday. Have dinner, take in a show, dance a little, have a whole weekend of fun. What do you think, Rachel—darling?''

CHAPTER FOUR

THEY WERE NOT THE FIRST to say good-night, but not the last, either. Rachel was worried about what other outrageous things Colin might say and so she seized the first respectable opportunity to make their farewells. Colin did not object. That didn't surprise her, but Rachel was frankly amazed that he didn't put on a show of being eager to have her to himself.

She made sure the butler was the one who helped her into her jacket. And though she didn't shrug off Colin's hand as he helped her into the car, because someone might be watching from the house, she didn't welcome his touch or look at him, either.

He started the car and waited a moment for the engine to warm while he pulled off his bow tie and released the collar of his shirt. "There, that's better. At least it wasn't as bad as Anne's usual parties."

Rachel made a brief noncommittal noise.

Colin shot a look at her. "Usually she has hordes of people and things go on forever," he explained.

Rachel said nothing.

Colin whistled something tuneless under his breath for several blocks. Finally, as they neared her house, he said, "You know how you get homicidal at jokes about short people? Well, I get the same way when I'm subjected to the silent treatment."

"Really?" Rachel's voice was cool. "Perhaps I'm not being silent because of you at all. I might be simply moody."

"Then blow up. Just don't sulk."

"I am not sulking, dammit!"

Colin eyed her with interest. "That's some improvement, but I'm sure you can do better if you let yourself go."

"I could have cheerfully brained you with the centerpiece!"

"Why?"

"For suggesting we go off for the weekend together like that!" As the little convertible turned into her driveway, she reached under the seat for the remote-control that opened the garage door.

"I didn't think it was such a bad idea." Colin groaned as he extricated himself from the driver's seat. "It might be fun. Besides, the last time I was there, Chicago still had more than one hotel room."

And no matter what the others at the dinner table tonight thought they had heard, Colin had never suggested they share one. Suddenly the utter foolishness of the exchange hit her, and she started to laugh. "All right. You get credit for that one. I must admit that the look on Anne's face..."

"It was worth it all, wasn't it? So, are we going to Chicago next Saturday?"

"It's still not a good idea, so my answer's still no. Thanks for taking me tonight, Colin." She unlocked the door and opened it. "Good night."

He shivered a little. "Can't I come in?"

No, she thought. That wasn't such a good idea, either.

He was watching her lips, and he seemed to see her refusal forming. "Not even to warm up before I get into another cold car?" he asked plaintively.

Rachel frowned. "Why aren't you wearing an overcoat?"

"You only specified that I rent a tux, not an—"

"You expect me to believe you *rented* that? I want to see the receipt."

"All right, I bought it. What was I supposed to do?" He followed her into the living room. "What kind of man do you think I am, Miss Todd? If I let you get away with renting my clothes, who knows what scandalous thing will be next? Red bikini underwear, no doubt. The rules say books and flowers and candy are the only appropriate gifts until an engagement is announced. And even then—"

"I know what the rules say, Colin. And don't expect me to believe you bought that tux today, either, or I'll throw you out on your ear."

He capitulated. "It was all those weddings. Much more economical in the long run. How about coffee? I'll even make it." He brushed by her and vanished into the kitchen.

Rachel sighed as she hung up her jacket and followed.

The coffee was already brewing by the time she entered the kitchen, and Colin was playing with the cat, who seemed fascinated by the gleam of pearl cuff links set in silver. "Do you ever let him go outside?" he asked.

"No. It seems cruel sometimes to keep him confined, but he'd already been declawed when I got him, so he couldn't defend himself. And since he's never been outside, I tell myself he doesn't really miss it. He has sunshine and fresh grass..." She waved a hand at a clay pot on the wide windowsill, where new green shoots sprang up. Part of the crop looked as if it had been chewed.

"Then there are the birds," Colin said.

"Yes. Cats hunt, whether they're hungry or not, and they don't show any discrimination or respect for endangered species."

"Well, think about it," Colin said reasonably. "Wouldn't a bluebird taste better than a sparrow?"

Bandit sank his teeth into the French cuff on Colin's shirt and shook his head as if trying to kill his prey.

"Cut it out, Bandit." Rachel reached into the cabinet for a neon-green plastic soda straw and held it out to the cat. Bandit's eyes widened and his tail switched menacingly. Rachel tossed the straw, and the cat was after it like a shot.

They took their coffee into the living room at Rachel's suggestion. She wouldn't have admitted it to Colin, but her kitchen felt uncomfortably small with him in it. There was something about formal clothes that made him seem to take up more room.

"I like the lived-in look," he said, with a glance at the half-full bookshelves.

"Right. Boxes still sitting around everywhere."

"I meant it," Colin protested. "It looks comfortable—books and wood and special things. All the place needs now is a fire."

Rachel shook her head. "I haven't gotten around to having the chimney cleaned yet. It might need it."

"That shouldn't be hard to check." He started toward the fireplace.

"Don't you dare—not in those clothes!"

"Oh. I forgot." He sat down, instead, and stretched out his feet toward the empty hearth. "It's your turn."

"For what?" Rachel curled up in the chair opposite him.

"Tell me about you."

"There's not much to tell."

"That's a feeble excuse, Rachel Todd. I learned more about you across the table tonight than I've been able to pry out of you in the last three days. It could have been mighty embarrassing if somebody had asked the wrong question—and sooner or later, they're bound to. How about some vital statistics? You can start with where and when you were born."

Rachel rolled her eyes. "Ann Arbor, Michigan. I'll be twenty-seven next month. My hair has always been too curly—"

"And red? I'll bet your baby pictures are cute."

"It's not red, it's auburn, and my eyes aren't brown, they're hazel. What else? Hobbies? I'm not bad at tennis, but I absolutely abhor golf." She sighed. "I haven't any idea what you want to know, Colin. This is ridiculous, anyway."

Colin's voice was gentle. "Just how young were you when your parents divorced?"

"Not quite two."

"Two?"

"You sound shocked."

"Then you don't even remember their being married, do you?"

Rachel gave up. The man was obviously not going to quit. "Furthermore, I don't remember my father at all. He moved—" she paused "—away, and I didn't see him for years."

"What did he do? Drill oil wells in the Middle East?"

"He was a professor of chemistry."

"Then he could have visited you regularly."

"I suppose he could have. He just never seemed to find time for things like that."

"Or for sending child-support checks, either, I suppose?" He shook his head. "That's why it was so tough for you to get through school, wasn't it?"

Rachel put her head back against the soft cushion of her chair. She was suddenly very tired. "You sound as if you know what it's like."

"No, I was very fortunate. Nicolet has an incredibly generous program for its employees. Their children get free tuition, and I lived at home till I graduated. Still, all of us were expected to earn the rest of our expenses, and I made things particularly hard for myself."

"How?"

"Flying lessons, and all that goes along with them, aren't cheap, but I wasn't about to stay grounded. I'd sooner have dropped out of school than quit flying."

"How did you get the money?"

Colin shrugged. "Whatever came along. I baby-sat, painted houses, shoveled snow. It was my choice, after all, so I never minded working for it. Then when I decided flying wasn't enough, I wanted to own the plane... But we're not going to start talking about me again, are we?"

Rachel gave him a rueful smile. "It was worth a try."

"So you grew up in Michigan," Colin prompted, "went to school there and started to work..."

"You're doing fine," she murmured. "Keep going and I'll let you know when you go astray." She closed her eyes.

Colin looked at her for several seconds. "And you fell in love," he said softly, "and he hurt you, and you ran to Arizona..."

Rachel sat up straight. "Wrong."

"Then why did you go?"

"For the professional challenge. It was a better job."

Colin didn't say anything, but he didn't look satisfied with the answer.

Rachel toyed with the gold nugget at her throat. She knew better than to ask, but she couldn't help herself. "Why do you insist there was a man who hurt me?"

"I'm not sure. Your father sounds like a skunk, that's true, but..." He shot a sideways glance at her as if he expected her to challenge the appraisal.

She didn't. She merely looked at him.

"But there's something more than that," he finished. "Something about you that isn't explained by your father's desertion. There's a question I'd really like to have answered, Rachel. Who's Carleton?"

"None of your business." The words were harsh, but her voice was soft, almost reluctant.

"Is he the man who hurt you?"

She shook her head.

"I'm glad." He drained his coffee cup. "I'd better go."

Rachel followed him to the door and leaned against the half wall that set the entry apart from the living room. "Why are you glad?"

"Because if someone once hurt you, you shouldn't owe him anything, or have to stay in touch. And this Carleton obviously has a lot of power where you're concerned."

She thought that over and smiled at him. "Don't worry. I can take care of myself."

"Something tells me you've always had to." He looked down at her for a long moment, and then his mouth brushed hers, a kiss as light and tentative as the one he'd given her when she was sitting in Dawn's car.

But this kiss seemed to linger on her lips long after he had gone.

RACHEL HAD FINISHED her note of thanks to the Garretts and was contemplating the incredible balance on her monthly credit-card statement when Colin arrived the next morning.

She put down her fountain pen and went to answer the door. He dropped a careless kiss on the tip of her nose, set a paper bag and a bulky wad of newspaper on the coffee table and started for the kitchen.

"Make yourself at home," Rachel called after him.

He grinned at her, the irony in her voice not lost on him. "Thanks, I will. Have a doughnut. Is there any coffee?"

"Not fresh. I wasn't expecting you for another hour."

"That's why I brought the paper. I thought we could see what's going on in Chicago next week."

"Remember? We're not going for the weekend. At least I'm not."

He poked his head back out of the kitchen. "You'd make me go alone?"

"You'll have company on the way back."

"Some company. Most of these jerks aren't the least bit sociable. They just sit in the back of the plane with their briefcases and shuffle papers. They think that speaking to the pilot is like being best friends with the janitor."

"They probably just don't want to distract you from matters of safety. Especially their safety."

Colin looked thoughtful. "Now, that *is* a consideration. You would be an awful distraction. Maybe you shouldn't go."

"If you're trying to use reverse psychology on me, you missed the mark, Colin." She put her bills and checkbook away, and when he brought the coffee to the living room she closed the rolltop desk and stood up. "What's appropriate dress for today?"

Colin ran an appreciative eye over her thigh-hugging jeans and soft pumpkin-colored sweater. "You look just fine to me."

Rachel told herself that the surge of warmth she felt was pure foolishness. She wasn't wearing a bit of makeup, and her hair was a wild tangle of curls because she'd simply run her fingers through it when she'd gotten out of the shower. "You're half-blind, too."

"I mean it. The only rules the McKennas consider are comfort and whatever they're doing after dinner. Which means Anne turns up in designer dresses and diamonds if she's got a fancy reception to attend, or worn-out jeans if she's been cleaning the garage."

Rachel considered that and decided she'd rather not dress in either extreme. Colin was wearing cords, but his shirt was as crisp as if it had just come out of the package, and his leather jacket was classier than an ordinary Windbreaker. A skirt and sweater should be safe, she thought.

He tugged a section out of the middle of the newspaper and thrust it at her. "Here. You're in charge of entertainment for the trip." He pulled a giant chocolate-covered doughnut from the paper bag he'd brought and propped his feet on the corner of the coffee table.

"Colin, honestly..." She turned the section right side up and released a low moan when she saw the cover story.

"What's the matter?"

"There's a new musical I'd like to see," Rachel admitted. "And it's just coming off Broadway and into Chicago."

He looked over her shoulder at the headline. "So we go. What's the big deal?"

"I am not going to stay overnight with you in Chicago, Colin."

"Well, that takes care of that, doesn't it?" He buried his head in the comic section.

Rachel read every word of the story about the new musical, dreaming of the special magic promised by the production.

I can still go, she told herself. It was foolish to think this was her only chance, or even her best one. Lakemont was only a three-hour drive from downtown Chicago. She could go there any weekend she chose. And she certainly didn't need a date to enjoy a musical!

She put the newspaper aside and went to change her clothes. It took a lot of deliberation before she chose a midcalf khaki skirt and a dark brown turtleneck, with chunky gold earrings and the gold-nugget necklace on a lengthier chain. Even then, she stared at herself in the mirror for a long time before she shrugged and decided it would have to do.

Colin looked up from the newspaper and blinked. "What kind of impression are you trying to make on my family, anyway?"

"A good one," Rachel snapped. "If you actually were serious about me, you'd hardly want me to show up looking like a bag lady, would you?"

"I certainly wouldn't want you to look uncomfortable."

"Well, I'm comfortable this way."

"Good." He walked around her slowly, inspecting every detail. "Then let's go."

In the yard next door, the same bunch of children she'd noticed the other day had raked up another big pile of leaves and were jumping into it from the nearest tree. Their gleeful shrieks drew Rachel's attention.

Colin opened her door. "You can't," he said. "You're too dressed up. I told you to wear your jeans."

She looked up at him in surprise. "How did you know I was even tempted?"

"The wistful look in your eyes. I had no idea you were that sort, Rachel darling."

"What sort?"

"The sort who likes to run and jump and romp with kids. I thought since you had no interest in men—"

"—that I couldn't possibly like kids, either? Sorry to break the news to you, but the two things don't necessarily have to go hand in hand. If I ever want kids of my own, I'll adopt some."

"There are easier ways," Colin drawled. "Or hasn't anybody ever told you the facts of life?"

Rachel put up her chin and ignored him.

"The silent treatment again?" he mused. "Maybe I'll change my tactics and get amorous, instead of homicidal."

"What?"

"I'll bet if I were to kiss you whenever you clam up, you'd soon start talking again."

"Maybe. But you wouldn't like what I'd have to say."

He smiled. "I'll take my chances."

The McKennas lived in an old neighborhood on the other side of the Nicolet campus. Rachel didn't quite know what she'd expected, but she was startled when the car turned into a narrow drive beside a tall old Queen

Anne house with an octagonal tower on one corner. It looked like every child's dream of where Grandma ought to live, Rachel thought, with an attic for rainy days and a big lawn to play in.

A tiny girl dropped from the spreading branches of a huge oak tree behind the house and came flying across the lawn to greet them, her blond pigtails bouncing as she ran.

"Is that the one you hit?" Rachel asked.

"The kid?"

"No, the tree. Remember your creative visualization?"

"Sure. That's the one. Of course it was a lot small—"

The child launched herself at him. Colin's breath went out in a whoosh, and he staggered under the sudden weight.

"Uncle Colin!" She gave him a cheeky grin. "See?"

Colin scratched his head in apparent puzzlement. "See what?" he asked and tugged at a pigtail. "Your new sweater? The ribbons in your hair?"

"Uncle Colin!" the child protested. Her big brown eyes were full of disappointment.

Rachel touched the child's cheek. "No front teeth?" she suggested. She was rewarded with a long stare, and then a slow smile.

"I like you," the child announced. "You notice things. Are you Uncle Colin's new girl?"

"Uh..." Rachel saw Colin's eyebrows lift and said firmly, "Yes, I am."

"That's nice. I heard Daddy tell Mommy that Uncle Colin had a new girl, and Mommy said she hoped that *this* time—"

"Rachel," Colin interrupted, "meet Susan, who is apparently going to take after her mother." He set the child down and she ran toward the house to relay the news of their arrival.

"And her mother is also your most esteemed sister-in-law," Rachel finished. "If the rest of the gauntlet is like this, I'm not sure I'm up to it."

"Oh, you've seen the worst of it. Mother never even notices who I bring, Dad doesn't care, and my grandmother is convinced that I'm..."

But whatever his grandmother thought was lost forever, because just then they stepped through the back door into a big kitchen full of noise and warmth and wonderful smells. A toddler came running over, his arms stretched upward. Susan reappeared with a book of fairy tales. Within seconds Colin was holding the little boy in his arms, and Susan was sitting on his feet, her arms locked around his knees.

Rachel studied the picture he presented and quoted him, with a hint of maliciousness in her voice. "I had no idea you were that sort, Colin."

"I certainly don't understand it," he said. "All I have to do is show up, and suddenly I'm drowning in urchins."

"I'll bet the kids in your neighborhood line up at your door to ask if you can come out and play."

"It's because he's never grown up himself," said a young woman in a pastel-colored maternity dress who was peeling potatoes at the kitchen sink. She dried her hands and held one out to Rachel. "Hello, I'm Camryn. And despite all the comments you'll hear flying around, Colin and I understand each other very well."

"She makes a terrific chocolate cake," Colin admitted.

"And whenever he stops being Peter Pan, he'll be a great father."

"When I want commercial endorsements, Camryn, I'll let you know. I don't see that I'm missing much, anyway. Anytime I feel an overwhelming desire to change a diaper, all I have to do is look around." He eyed the child in his arms. "And sure enough, there's always one needing changing."

Camryn sighed. "I can't believe I'm going to have two in diapers for the next year at least. I ought to have my head examined." She took the toddler, who wailed his disapproval at being moved, from Colin's arms and carried him out of the room.

"One down," Colin said cheerfully. "Now if I can just peel the other one loose we'll go find Mother and Dad and get that bit over with."

It was not the ordeal Rachel had feared. She found Colin's mother to be nearly as vague as he'd described her, but utterly charming. And she fell in love with Professor McKenna, who was obviously the source not only of his children's characteristic dark hair and blue eyes, but their incredibly warm smiles, as well. She could have settled right down in his book-lined study and discussed the finer points of mathematics for days.

Talking about math would have been less stressful than helping with dinner preparations, that was for sure. Although not even Camryn made another suggestive comment, Rachel's anticipation of one had her feeling strung with wires by the time dinner was over and the cleanup was complete. When Anne proposed that the two of them take a walk, Rachel looked around wildly for Colin. He was nowhere to be seen.

Anne had not missed the desperation in Rachel's eyes. As they set off, she said bluntly, "He's out in the garage fixing the faulty starter on Dad's snowblower. In any case, you don't need him to be a guard dog. This is not one of those heart-to-heart girl talks."

"It isn't?" Rachel said feebly.

"I already had one of those with Camryn and told her to lay off. It's not fair to you."

They were halfway down the block before Rachel found her voice. "That was very thoughtful of you."

"No, it's not. I just wish I knew what Colin was up to. He's made it very clear that he's not interested in settling down, and if he's leading you on..."

"Of course he's not." It was out before Rachel could stop herself.

The only sound for several seconds was the clicking of the heels of Anne's boots against the sidewalk. "I think I'm beginning to see the light," she said thoughtfully. "Colin's certainly not serious. But you aren't, either, are you?"

Rachel swallowed hard. "It was sort of your idea."

"Mine?" Anne sounded horrified.

"You said if I wasn't so militant about not wanting to date, people would leave me alone. So I thought if I pretended to be seeing someone... So far, it's working." They walked on a little in silence. "You don't mind, do you, Anne?"

"Mind? Heavens, no. It's not my business. Just how long do you expect to carry on this little..." She paused.

"Fraud?" Rachel finished. "Just till Thanksgiving."

"Oh. I see."

Rachel looked at her anxiously. "You won't tell the others, will you?"

"Of course not. I've suffered through so many well-meaning comments in the past couple of years about when I'm going to start a family that frankly I—"

Colin came around the corner, jogging. "There you are," he said with relief and dropped into step between them.

"Don't worry," Anne said. "I wasn't reenacting the Spanish Inquisition on her."

He grinned at her. "You're the very best of sisters, Annie, and I appreciate it."

"I'm your *only* sister, Colin."

"That, too. We have to run, Rachel. A photographer friend of mine needs to shoot aerial pictures this afternoon."

"Don't you ever plan ahead, Colin?" Rachel asked.

He shook his head. "You can't plan for things like this. It depends on the weather and the amount of haze in the air. Do you want to come with me, or stay here till I get back?"

They turned the corner and walked the last hundred yards toward the house. Rachel could see what looked like a horseshoe-pitching session on the front lawn.

Great, she thought. Either I go with him, or I get kissed goodbye in front of the whole clan.

"How long will you be?" she asked.

"An hour or so."

"Don't believe it," Anne warned. "When he gets in the air he has no sense of time."

"How about taking me home first?" Rachel suggested.

Colin shook his head. "Can't. We're half an hour from the airport, and by the time we get a plane up the shadows will be starting to lengthen."

"Then I guess I'll go."

"That's my girl—always ready for any challenge."

Hasty goodbyes were the easiest kind, Rachel discovered. There was no chance for private comments, or even winks and smiles. And no time for questions about when she might come again.

On the way to the airport, Rachel said, "Silly me. I thought when I saw you jogging toward us that you were coming to my rescue."

"Sorry, but I left my white horse at home today. Besides, there wasn't any need to rescue you from Anne. She's one of the good guys. She'd never let me down."

"Well, I'm glad you trust her. She's figured out what we're up to."

"What?"

Rachel looked at him warily, a little surprised by his vehemence. "I should have warned you, I suppose, that it was Anne who gave me the bit of advice I told you about."

He frowned and then said, "On dealing with matchmakers by dating so you don't have to date? Yes, that does sound like Anne, now that I think about it." He didn't seem very happy.

"I can't help it, you know. That happened before I even met you—the second time, I mean, at the ice-cream parlor. But perhaps I should warn you that Anne's not the only one who's on to you."

Colin shot her a look that was positively dangerous. "Oh?"

"I didn't do a thing to bring this on," Rachel said. "I am completely innocent. Your grandmother told me that she hoped I wasn't serious about you, because you weren't about to give up your freedom."

"Oh, that's nothing new. Nell's been saying that about me since I was six. At least she isn't trying to marry me off, thank God."

Rachel glared at him. "I wouldn't be so sure of that. She gave me some advice, just in case I want to go after you."

"Nell? You're kidding."

"She suggested if I wanted to hold your attention, I should dab jet fuel behind my ears instead of perfume."

He shot her a look of pure amazement and then burst out laughing. "Oh, Lord, I hope Camryn didn't hear that one," he gasped. "She'll start giving out bottles of the stuff for Christmas!"

CHAPTER FIVE

THE AIRPLANE waiting for them outside the charter terminal of the Lakemont airport was not the one Rachel had expected to see. It was a red-and-silver single-engine model, little more than a capsule suspended beneath a pair of wings. To Rachel, who'd been on nothing smaller than the ten-passenger turboprop, this one looked no bigger—and no more substantial—than a toy.

She trailed Colin as he walked around the plane making his preflight inspection. "Do you own this, too?" she asked.

He nodded, but didn't take his eyes off the aircraft. "We've got several this size. This one is usually leased out by the month, so we're lucky it's in right now."

"You mean it's like a rental car?"

She could see the way his eyes crinkled at the corners, and she knew, despite the dark glasses he wore, he was regarding her with that sparkle of unholy glee she had seen him display more than once. "What's the matter? Are you afraid some careless driver has been hot-rodding it?"

"Well, a mile up in the air is no place to find out."

"Cheer up. These are strictly low-level photos. Half a mile, tops."

She thought about that for a minute as he strode on around the plane. Rachel had to run to catch up. "That's supposed to comfort me? I think I'll just stay here on the ground."

"Why? Don't you trust me to get you back in one piece?"

"It's not that, Colin. I've just never flown in anything so small before."

"Then you are in for a treat. In you go—you have the whole back seat to yourself. Jon needs the front so he can shoot." He frowned. "Too bad I didn't think of it earlier. We should have brought Susan."

Reluctantly Rachel stepped onto the tiny foothold on the wing strut, then paused. "For her first flight? That would be sweet."

Colin put both hands on her derriere and pushed. Rachel's eyes widened in shock, and she hastily pulled herself up to the airplane's door.

"Heck, no," he said. "She's a veteran. She could have comforted you."

She slid into the back seat and said to no one in particular, "Last night he was complaining about my car. There's more room in it than in this thing, that's for sure. And more protection in case of a collision, too."

"What are you muttering about? Here, you'd better take my coat." He handed the leather jacket to her and climbed into the pilot's seat.

"Why?"

"Because it gets colder the higher we go. And Jon will have the window open, so the breeze will be—"

"He's going to open the window?" Rachel howled. "I want to stay down here!"

But the photographer, laden with bags of equipment, had already climbed in, and a moment later the engine roared to life. Rachel closed her eyes, trying to remember everything she'd ever been told about crash positions. Not that it would do any good in this tuna can, she reminded herself.

She felt a little better, however, when the minutes dragged on and the plane was still standing, while Colin checked every gauge and dial and moving part. Unless, the pessimistic part of her warned, he'd found something that wasn't quite up to par and was trying to figure out how to make it work right...

"Don't worry," Colin said over his shoulder. "I'm sure I told the mechanic to fix the loose wing."

Rachel stuck her tongue out at him. He only smiled.

She felt every bump and seam on the concrete taxiway, and near the end of the runway, as they waited for permission to take off, she could feel the plane shuddering under the strain of the opposing forces of engine and brakes. It was not a comforting sensation.

The radio crackled to life, but the voice that came across the airwaves was so full of static that Rachel couldn't make out a word. Colin obviously could, for he answered, and then they were off, hurtling down the runway and then easing into the sky.

To Rachel it felt more as if they were holding steady while the earth fell away in slow motion. It was like nothing she'd ever experienced before.

She'd spent her share of time in jet airliners, and on a cloudless day had experienced the breathtaking sensation of looking down from thirty thousand feet and seeing the curve of the earth in the hazy horizon. But usually at that altitude she felt isolated, shut away from the world by distance and clouds, as if what she was watching through a tiny pane of scratched glass was only a movie.

This was a different sort of magic. She had a sense of being able to reach down and move the cars and trains and villages as if they were toys and she was Gulliver in the land of the Lilliputians. And she experienced an incredible sensuality, too, as if she was actually a part of the aircraft, feeling every vibration and shudder and change in altitude as the air currents slapped against the little plane.

When Jon opened the window, the cold wind streaming through her hair made her gasp. Colin glanced over his shoulder. "Hold on. There should be an airsickness bag back there."

Rachel shook her head. "I'm fine." She had to shout over the combined roar of the engine and wind. "But if this is what being a bird is like, I'd never leave the nest!"

He smiled but didn't answer, and put the plane into a tight turn. Rachel gazed through the window beside her straight down at the roof of a building and thought for a moment it might be too late to look for the bag he'd mentioned. Then the sensation passed and the fascination reasserted itself, and she pressed her nose against the glass for a better look. When Jon finally closed the window, she was almost disappointed at the sudden calm.

"Got it," the photographer said.

Colin nodded, and the plane leveled out and cruised slowly back toward the airport.

Rachel was still shivering a little, so she huddled into Colin's jacket. The mouton collar, soft and curly, tickled her nose. Or was it the faint aroma of his after-shave, mixed with the scent of the leather, that tugged at her senses?

They circled the airport for a few minutes, waiting their turn. Then the wheels kissed the pavement with a screech, and the magic was over.

The photographer climbed out and headed toward the parking lot. Then Colin got out. Rachel extricated herself from the back seat and paused in the doorway to judge how best to reach the tiny foothold. It hadn't been too bad going up, but her low-heeled pumps didn't leave margin for error.

"Your friend is certainly a man of few words," she said.

Grabbing her around the waist, Colin swung her down beside him and into a sort of bear hug. If Rachel hadn't braced her hands against his shoulders to steady herself, she'd have fallen flat against him.

But even after she had regained her balance, Colin didn't let her go. "This is one of the nicest things about flying, I've always thought," he mused, and his hands slid slowly upward from her waist.

Rachel planted both her hands on his chest and shoved, with no appreciable effect. Colin laughed and released her. "Let me finish the paperwork, and I'll buy you a drink to recuperate. Have you been to Brannigan's?"

Rachel had heard of the Irish pub, located in the old commercial district of the city not far from the shore of Lake Michigan, but she'd never been there. Once inside she gazed around with astonishment. "It looks authentic," she said. The room was low and dim and plain. Nothing in the whole place could have been called ornate, but each piece of wood in the place was worn beautifully smooth with use and polishing. There was a fireplace off to one side of the bar. A couple of tall wooden stools stood in the center of a small space that might have been a dance floor. Atop one of them a banjo was balanced.

"Oh, it's completely authentic. It was purchased lock, stock and beer strainers and moved here from Dublin a hundred years ago." Colin's pager beeped, and he grimaced and pointed out a table. "I'll be right back."

The bar was crowded, and Rachel was surprised when a waitress came right over. "What would you like, ma'am?"

"I'll wait till my..." Rachel paused. What *was* he to her, anyway? "Boyfriend" was such a silly word.

"Oh, I know what Colin wants."

Rachel studied the waitress with interest. "In that case, I'll have an Irish coffee. And can I pay for these now, before he comes back?"

The waitress smiled and shrugged. "Colin won't like it, but it certainly doesn't matter to me."

Rachel dug out her wallet. "Keep the change. Are you and Colin friends?"

The waitress eyed the denomination of the bill with appreciation. "Not the way you mean. But we get to know the regulars around here."

That was interesting, Rachel thought. A regular at an Irish pub who swore he never touched alcohol. And it was also intriguing, she told herself, that the waitress had automatically assumed she was jealous.

Colin pulled out the chair next to her. "It was nothing important. Is Peggy taking care of you?"

The waitress returned with their drinks, a steaming tall mug for Rachel, a can of ginger ale and a glass of ice for Colin. He reached for his money clip.

"The drinks are sort of on the house," Peggy said, and winked at Rachel.

Rachel sipped her Irish coffee and met Colin's gaze over the edge of the glass mug. "Why are you looking suspiciously at me?" she asked politely.

"Because the last time Brannigan's gave away a drink was sometime before the turn of the century." He poured his ginger ale into the ice-filled glass. "Well? Did you hate flying in a small plane as much as you expected?"

"I didn't hate it. In fact..." She hesitated, feeling foolish. What had been going through her mind was just a silly passing thought, not worth sharing.

"Come on. Anything that makes you turn that delicate shade of pink must be interesting enough to share."

And if she didn't tell him, he'd probably speculate and come up with something far wilder than the truth. She drew circles on the wooden tabletop with the base of her mug. "If I wanted to take flying lessons, how would I do it?"

Colin choked on his first sip of ginger ale. "You're kidding."

"Not exactly. I haven't made up my mind, of course, I'm only thinking about it."

"Right." His voice was dry.

Rachel stared at him and felt heat rise in her face. "And I'm not bringing it up to impress you, either."

"That idea never occurred to me."

"Oh, forget the whole thing! I just thought it might be kind of interesting, that's all." She picked up her mug. Her hand was shaking, partly from embarrassment but mostly in fury at him for being so egotistical. Even if she wanted him, which she emphatically didn't, she wouldn't be so stupidly transparent as to take that route to get his attention!

Colin leaned back in his chair. "Well, if you want to give it a try, you should start by talking nicely to your favorite pilot."

"You?"

"You have others?" he countered.

"You could teach me?"

"I'm a licensed instructor, yes. It fills in some dead time. Airplanes don't make any money when they're sitting on the ground." His voice softened. "Would you really like to learn, Rachel?"

She studied the random pattern of the cinnamon sprinkled on the whipped cream of the coffee. "Maybe," she said.

"Damn. If I'd known that, I'd have shown you a few maneuvers. You know—barrel rolls, stall-outs, some interesting stuff. But I was trying to fly that thing like a baby carriage so you wouldn't be too upset."

Her eyes widened. "That was your idea of smooth flying? You were standing that plane on its wing!"

"Well," he said mildly, "it's always a bit of a challenge to get the camera where it needs to be without a wing strut in the way. Flying for aerial photos is not an occupation for amateurs. So, when do you want to begin?"

"I'm only thinking about it, Colin. Don't start counting your lesson fees just yet."

"For you, Rachel, honey, I would never charge a fee."

"What kind of businessman are you?"

"A terrible one," Colin said promptly. "I wouldn't even charge you for the fuel."

Before Rachel could answer, three young men approached the tall stools on the dance floor. Two carried acoustic guitars, the other picked up the banjo and began to strum. The guitars joined in, and the rhythmic strumming gave way to a soft haunting melody.

Rachel checked her watch. "I've never heard of a bar with entertainment on Sunday afternoons."

"You don't suppose Brannigan's has survived for a century by being just like every other bar, do you? Enjoy the show."

Peggy appeared, her tray held high to avoid the crowd, with another round of drinks. She set another ginger ale in front of Colin and swept Rachel's empty mug away, replacing it with a steaming one. "This one's on me, too," the waitress said when Colin protested.

He did not give in easily, and Peggy finally stopped him by simply disappearing into the crowd. He settled back into his chair with a disgusted sigh.

"Why all the fuss?" Rachel said mildly. "Obviously you're a very special customer." She wasn't about to admit that Peggy was obviously still operating on the money she'd given her.

"She can't afford that kind of gesture," he muttered.

Rachel raised her eyebrows.

"She works two jobs to support herself." He gave his ginger-ale can a push. "She doesn't need to be doing things like this."

Rachel licked whipped cream from her upper lip. "Of course not, but why fight about it if it makes her feel good?" she asked reasonably. "It's not polite to remind her that she's poverty-stricken. Just leave her a nice tip to make up for it. What is that song? I thought Irish music consisted of 'Danny Boy' and 'When Irish Eyes Are Smiling.'"

Colin smiled, but the shadow didn't quite leave his eyes.

Rachel found it fascinating. She took a long look at Peggy, waiting on a table full of men across the bar. The woman had indicated there wasn't anything special between her and Colin, and yet, if he was so concerned . . .

"'Danny Boy'? You've got a lot to learn about Irish music," Colin said, and started teaching her the lyrics. The next hour passed in a blur of one lively song after another, and soon Rachel was singing along.

"You've got a really good voice for this sort of thing," Colin told her. "Are you certain you're not Irish?"

"You couldn't prove it by me," she said carelessly. "I haven't any idea what I am."

By the time Colin took her home it was very late.

"I had a wonderful time," she said gleefully as he unlocked her front door. "And I'm not telling a sociable white lie, either."

"I know." He looked a little worried. "I've never seen anyone get so high on just a couple of Irish coffees."

She leaned against the door and looked up at him. "It wasn't the Irish coffees. It was the laughter and the music..." She started to hum a minor-key ballad.

His eyes softened. "Good Lord, girl, have you never had any fun before?"

She didn't answer. Instead, she stood on her tiptoes and let her fingertips rest on his chest for balance, then she kissed the corner of his mouth. "Thank you, Colin," she whispered.

She would have ducked into the house and closed the door, but she'd miscalculated the length of his reach. His hands closed on her shoulders, and he almost dragged her back into the doorway.

For a moment she couldn't look at him. She was too embarrassed. What had made her do that? Kissing him had been a silly thing to do, silly and pointless.

And completely innocent, too. Why shouldn't she thank him? It had been the most enjoyable day she'd had in a long time. And it wasn't as if that kiss had been anything out of the ordinary; it was just the simple brush of the lips that friends exchanged all the time.

She raised her eyes to his and started to tell him that, if her kiss had bothered him, she was sorry. And so, her lips were already slightly parted when his arms tightened around her and he bent his head.

Her eyes widened a little, but there was no time for a protest before his mouth was on hers, warm and gentle.

Rachel had not known that a simple kiss could be a three-act play in miniature. Colin began by nibbling her lower lip, creating a pleasant sort of itch she'd never experienced before, a sensation relieved only when he stopped nibbling and settled down to seriously kissing her. Colin's kiss was firm and mobile and tantalizing, and he tasted sweet. This was not the breath-robbing teeth-grinding sort she had experienced on occasion; this kind of kiss could go on forever....

Finally he let his tongue flick playfully against the corners of her mouth and raised his head. "There," he said. "Now that's the proper way to say thank-you."

He sounded a little out of breath. No surprise, she thought. She felt short of oxygen herself.

"I'll remember the lesson," she said. Her voice sounded very small.

Colin laughed. "You do that, Rachel, honey."

He left her standing in the doorway, leaning against the jamb. She was glad of it, because her ankles seemed to have dissolved and she wouldn't have liked him to see her trying to learn to walk all over again. Foolishness, she thought. Pure foolishness. Why had he done such a thing, anyway?

But on the other hand, why shouldn't she let Colin kiss her now and then if he wanted? This wasn't serious, any of it. So why shouldn't they have a little fun along the way?

And Colin certainly could be fun....

RACHEL WAS WITH A STUDENT Tuesday morning, going over the newest set of instructions for financial-aid forms, when her secretary buzzed her on the intercom. "Mr. McKenna insists that you will want to talk to him," Amy said, "no matter how busy you are. I told him you were with a student and he said—"

Rachel could imagine what he had said. "Never mind. I'll give him two minutes." She glanced at the student. "If you'll excuse me, please." She picked up the phone.

Colin said pleasantly, "Good morning, sweetheart. This fixation of yours with students worries me."

"Is that what you called to tell me?"

"No. I just have one word to say to you this morning. 'Matinee.'"

"What?"

"To be more specific, Sunday matinee."

She gasped. "The musical? Will we have time?"

"I found out just this morning that our passenger is taking the last possible flight out of Atlanta, so we can go to the show and still have time to kill before we pick him up."

Rachel's eyes were aglow. "That's wonderful! I'll call and get the tickets right away."

She knew from the sound of his voice that Colin was smiling. "Fair enough. See you later."

She was late meeting Dawn for lunch because the ticket office was so busy she'd been on hold for more than half an hour. "Sorry," she gasped as she settled into a booth at the ice-cream parlor across the street. She couldn't help recalling that it was the same booth she'd been sitting in that rainy night when she'd run into Colin. "I had to make a phone call."

Dawn stopped picking at her chicken salad. "To Crash, no doubt?"

"Please, Dawn. If you'd ever flown with him, you wouldn't call him that."

"And obviously you have flown with him."

"Of course," Rachel said lightly. "I told you I met him on the Minneapolis trip."

"That's funny. The only man I remember you mentioning after that outing was Ted Lehmann."

"Oh, well, you don't expect me to tell all my secrets, do you?" She glanced at the menu and looked around for the waitress, who appeared almost instantly. "I'd like a club sandwich on rye and a glass of iced tea," she said absently, and then realized that the waitress looked familiar. "Peggy? Is this your other job?"

The young woman nodded. "Here during the week, Brannigan's on weekends." She was gone before Rachel could say another word.

"You know the strangest people, Rachel." Dawn pushed the remains of her salad away. "I have to run— got a class." She pulled her jacket off the back of her seat and smiled. "You know, we really should have lunch together someday."

After she was gone, Rachel shrugged. "Sorry, Dawn," she muttered under her breath. But if she had to choose between spending a half hour over lunch with Dawn or snagging two of the most sought-after tickets in the city of Chicago, she'd take the tickets every time. In fact, the knowledge that those two tickets were waiting for her, safely charged to her credit card and tucked away at the box office, was enough to send tremors of pure delight through her body.

Peggy returned with Rachel's sandwich and tea, then removed Dawn's discarded dishes.

"Do you like your work?" Rachel asked.

Peggy's eyes flicked over the table, making sure it was as neat as she could make it. "It'll do till I get something better."

"What's the something better you're hoping for?" The lunch rush was over and the shop was clearing out, so perhaps Peggy had a minute to chat. Besides, it wasn't simply an idle question; though Rachel didn't exactly want to admit it, she was curious as to what there was about this young woman that made Colin like her so much.

Peggy began to clear the nearby tables. "Child psychology. If I ever manage to get through the preliminaries, that is."

Rachel's eyebrows rose a little in surprise. "Are you studying now?"

"I take a class whenever I can manage it at the community college downtown."

"You can't get a degree in child psychology from the community college, can you? They've only got a two-year program."

Peggy shook her head tiredly. "I'll have to figure out a way to go on somewhere else. But that's a long way off at the rate I'm going."

Rachel looked at her thoughtfully for a moment and said, "I'd like to talk to you about it."

A couple of people came in, laughing and talking, and settled at a table that hadn't yet been cleared.

"Sorry, but I have to work my tables," Peggy said.

"I know. I didn't mean just now." Rachel pulled her business card out of her handbag. "Come to my office some time this week."

Peggy glanced at the card and looked up with a frown. "I've talked to counselors before, Miss Todd. It didn't do any good. With my two jobs, I make just a little too much money to get help—and not quite enough to save anything.''

''I don't make the rules, Peggy. But once in a while I can find a way to bend them.''

''You mean Nicolet would...'' Peggy's eyes shone for an instant, then she shook her head. ''Not a chance. Do you know what that costs?'' She looked down at Rachel's card again and smiled ruefully. ''Sorry, stupid question. Of course you know.''

''Come and see me.''

Peggy didn't answer, but she put the card into her apron pocket along with her tips before she went to clear the table for the newcomers.

It would be interesting, Rachel thought, to see if Peggy appeared. She wouldn't care to bet on it either way, however.

By Thursday, she'd almost given up on her. But that morning when she came into the administration building, shivering from the first really frosty morning of the fall, Rachel almost fell over the woman sitting just inside the financial-aid office.

''I'm sorry to be so early,'' Peggy said. ''But I have to work an extra shift today, so...''

''Come right in and we'll get started.'' Rachel hung up her coat, blew on her hands to warm them and pulled a folder of blank forms out of her secretary's file drawer.

Peggy eyed the papers with distaste and she uncapped her pen. ''I don't even know why I'm here,'' she muttered. ''It seems as if these days you have to be flat broke and on welfare to qualify for financial aid, or else wealthy enough to pay cash for an education. The people in the middle, who are making a living but want to do better for themselves, can't get any help at all.''

"That's probably true at the community college. But here, where costs are so much higher, about sixty percent of our students get some kind of financial aid."

Peggy's pen didn't stop moving across the forms. "That's nice, but it's still going to cost more than I can afford, I bet."

Rachel occupied herself with paperwork. Normally she would have suggested Peggy take the application to the outer office, but something told her if the woman got that far she might just keep on walking.

Finally Peggy read the questions one last time, reconsidered a couple of answers, then passed the form across the desk with a sigh. "I don't mean to fuss, Miss Todd, honestly I don't. I appreciate your taking the time to help me. But . . ."

"But perhaps you're afraid to get your hopes up?"

Peggy nodded and said very quietly, "I want it so badly, you see."

They talked for a long time, and after Peggy left, Rachel sat for another half hour studying the application and thinking.

Then she picked up the telephone and dialed an unlisted number—a number so private that, instead of letting it show up on the university's telephone bill, she charged the call to her personal credit card.

When it was answered, she said quietly, "Roger? This is Rachel. I've got a name for you."

THE USHER TOOK the precious tickets from Colin's hand, glanced at the numbers and said, "This way, sir. I'll show you to your seats."

The farther he led them down the center aisle toward the front of the theater, the more thoughtful Colin became. As they sat down, he said quietly, "Aisle seats, six rows from the front? Where did you hit the gold mine, Rachel?''

''Amazing things, credit cards,'' she said lightly.

''Yeah, but you still have to pay for what you charge.'' He helped her out of her fur jacket. ''These must be the best seats in the house.''

''Not quite. The best ones were already taken.'' She grinned. ''Do you worry about everybody's finances, Colin? First it was Peggy, now it's me.''

''Peggy's a nice kid. I hate seeing her work herself to death that way and make no progress.'' He shook a finger at her. ''She confessed, by the way, that you gave her the money for the drinks last weekend, so actually that makes this little outing my turn.''

''We can argue about the bill later. Just relax and enjoy, all right?''

The houselights dimmed and the overture began with a crashing thunderous chord. Rachel settled back and snuggled into her coat.

''Like a kitten,'' Colin said. ''You're just like a—''

''Shut up, or I'll wish I hadn't brought you.''

He smiled and didn't say another word. But he held her hand through both acts, only letting go at intermission.

It was almost dark by the time they came out of the theater. Rachel could hardly talk; the sheer beauty of the music had left her spellbound.

''That was wonderful, wasn't it?'' she managed as they waited by the cabstand.

''Not bad,'' Colin conceded.

Rachel punched him in the arm.

He grinned at her and pulled off his tie, folded it carefully and tucked it into the pocket of his blazer. ''In fact, anytime you want to do it again, just give me a call, honey.''

They ate juicy burgers at a dark little dive in the Loop, and by the time the shuttle bus delivered them to the terminal at O'Hare it was almost time for their passenger's flight to arrive from Atlanta.

"What's this guy coming in for, anyway?" Rachel asked as they waited at the gate.

"Job interview, I guess."

"What kind of job?"

"How should I know? I only ferry the passengers, I don't read their résumés."

He charmed the ticket agent out of a sheet of cardboard and set about making a sign so the passenger could spot them.

"Why didn't you fly in to get me when I came up for my interview?" Rachel asked. "I had to take the commuter airline."

Colin didn't even look up. "Rachel, honey, if I'd had any idea what I was missing, I'd have been here in a minute, orders or no orders."

She laughed and looked over his shoulder. Her face froze when she saw the name he was writing on his makeshift sign.

She told herself not to be ridiculous. There were thousands of men named Hamilton in the world. And certainly the one she knew didn't hail from Atlanta.

Passengers began streaming along the ramp from the jetliner, and Colin held up his sign. Within a couple of minutes, a man with a garment bag over his shoulder broke off from the crowd and strode toward them.

Rachel's stomach dropped to her toes.

"Well, hello, Rachel," Derek Hamilton said easily. "I hoped to see you, of course, but I never dreamed you'd make it a point to meet me. Am I to conclude that you've missed me all these lonely months? What a lovely idea!"

CHAPTER SIX

IT TOOK ALL the self-control Rachel could muster to respond politely. "Hello, Derek. Did you have a good flight?"

His eyes had a strange gleam she had long ago learned to distrust. "Not nearly as good as the landing turned out to be."

She didn't look at Colin, but she knew he was watching her. His voice was clipped as he asked Derek, "Do you have any luggage to pick up?"

"Just this."

Derek handed him the garment bag as if Colin was a porter. Fury rose in Rachel's throat, and she had to damp it down, otherwise she'd have kicked Derek Hamilton in the kneecap. There was no point in making a scene. She ought to introduce them, she supposed. At least then Derek would realize he wasn't dealing with a flunky.

She drew a breath to do so just as Derek reached for her arm. "Let's get going, all right?" he said.

Colin eyed him coolly. Then he dropped the cardboard sign into the nearest trash bin and shifted Derek's garment bag to his other hand. "Yes, sir," he murmured. "This way, sir." He strode off toward the entrance and the shuttle bus that would take them to the charter terminal.

Rachel bit her lip. Nothing as simple as an introduction would do any good now. Even if she could make Derck realize how rude he was being, he probably wouldn't care. And Colin was obviously in no mood to overlook the insults; she and Derek practically had to run to keep up with him.

At the charter terminal, the sleek turboprop was already refueled and waiting. Colin hung the garment bag up in a cupboard in the cabin and without another word went back out into the night. He was going to make his visual inspection of the plane, Rachel supposed, or file their flight plan, or check on the weather. She didn't know and she didn't care, as long as he didn't dawdle. The quicker they got back to Lakemont, the sooner she could talk to him.

Derek was looking around the cabin, compact and quietly comfortable. "Not bad," he conceded. "I must admit I didn't expect anything quite this nice."

"Nicolet doesn't own it." She turned back to the doorway. "Make yourself comfortable. I'll be back in a minute."

"Are you going to scold the pilot? The service does leave a little to be desired."

How, she asked herself, could I ever have thought he was charming, or caring, or understanding?

She caught up with Colin at the tail of the plane. He knew she was there, that was obvious, but he didn't take his eyes off the equipment.

"I'm sorry he was so rude," Rachel said quietly. "He's—"

"Not normally like that?" Colin's tone was skeptical.

Rachel tried to smile. "Well, I wouldn't go that far."

"What is he, anyway? Your ex-husband?" Colin said over his shoulder as he moved toward the wing.

"No! Oh, no." Rachel scrambled to follow.

"Current husband, then?"

"Of course not."

"Old boyfriend?"

"I suppose that's the most accurate description."

"And you want him back."

She shook her head vehemently.

"Well, that's the only reason I can see for the sudden change in your attitude, Rachel. You went from 'Colin, you're such a sweetheart to think of the matinee' to 'James, bring round the car, please,' in less time than—"

"I didn't say a word!"

"You didn't have to."

She gulped, and a tear dropped silently onto the soft sleeve of her jacket and lay balanced against the fur. She stared at it as if taking her eyes off the perfect little droplet would bring her whole world crashing down. "I'm sorry," she managed. "I just thought it would be better if he didn't have any reason to wonder about...us."

"Why? What could he possibly do about it?"

He could make things very uncomfortable for me, Rachel thought. But she could hardly expect Colin to understand how truly vindictive Derek was capable of being. She shrugged wearily and turned back toward the aircraft.

Derek patted the empty seat beside him. Instead, Rachel took the facing seat, a single that backed on the bulkhead between cabin and cockpit, and fastened her seat belt with a snap.

"Sure you don't want to share?" he asked.

"Absolutely certain." She stared out the window, imagining what the view would be at takeoff as the lights of Chicago dropped away beneath them. But the window was small, and it wouldn't give her any idea at all what the scenery would be from the cockpit.

She had looked forward to seeing that. On the flight down, Colin had described the city at night. A golden net of light, he had said, like gleaming beads strung on vast spiderwebs.

And now she was going to miss it, because Derek was here and she was in the cabin, instead of in the copilot's seat.

Rachel reached into the side pocket of her handbag for a tissue, and her fingertips brushed the ticket stubs. Tears sprang to her eyes. All the magic she and Colin had shared today was gone, spoiled, because of the man who sat across from her.

"What brought you here, anyway?" Her voice was low.

"What makes any of us hopscotch around the country trying to better ourselves?" Derek countered. "Nicolet's looking for a vice president of student affairs. Bigger school, better salary, more responsibility."

"And you just happened to decide to apply?"

He studied her for a moment. "Would it do me any good if I told you I'd followed you?"

"No."

"You wouldn't believe me?"

"No. But even if that's true, it doesn't matter."

The plane rocked slightly as Colin climbed aboard. "Mr. Hamilton," he said, "I need to go over some safety procedures."

Derek waved a hand impatiently. "Oh, for heaven's sake, man, do you expect to have to ditch this bird in the lake? I've been in small planes before. It's late and I've got better things to do. Let's just get in the air, all right?''

Colin didn't seem inclined to argue. He turned to Rachel, instead. She could feel the weight of his gaze, but she didn't look up; she didn't want to see the chill in his face.

''Aren't you game for another lesson?'' he asked.

His voice was gentle, almost chiding, and Rachel's eyes raised in surprise to meet his. He wasn't angry anymore? And what did he mean, *another* lesson? She'd never had a first one. Ah, of course. Colin was offering her a plausible excuse to escape to the cockpit, without Derek's suspecting there might be some other reason for her move.

She unfastened her seat belt. ''Sure, I'm game.''

Derek looked horrified. ''You're going to let her fly this plane? I'll report you to your boss.''

Colin paused in the doorway between cockpit and cabin. ''Do that,'' he said genially. The click of the door closing seemed oddly final.

Colin didn't hesitate; his hands moved surely from switch to switch, and the engines roared into life. Rachel looked at the controls that surrounded her with a new trepidation. On the flight down, she'd scarcely paid any attention to the dials and gauges and levers; she'd been too busy watching the view.

''You're not serious about a lesson, are you?'' Her voice shook just a little.

''Instrument flying at night when you've never had a yoke in your hands before?'' His tone was dry. ''That would be like putting a novice driver down in the middle of the Grand Prix. I'm not suicidal, Rachel.''

The lights of the city were all he had promised. In fact, the skein of gold stretched all the way up the shore of Lake Michigan. In some places it was a narrow dense band, and in others a wide-flung net of light. The beauty of it caught at Rachel's throat, and she was so absorbed in the show that she almost forgot the reason for the flight.

Finally Colin said, "I gather you knew our passenger in Arizona?"

Rachel nodded.

"What was he doing in Atlanta, then?"

"I didn't ask him. Maybe he got a special price on his ticket that way." She caught the skeptical look Colin shot at her and sighed. "I dated him for a while. He was the vice president of student affairs at the college I worked for."

"And the two of you had a quarrel, and you ran. I think I see."

"You don't see anything, Colin. It was over months before I decided to come to Nicolet."

"And that explains the way you reacted when you saw him." His voice was bland.

It didn't explain anything, and Rachel knew it. But before she could make up her mind what to tell him, Colin was talking to the air-traffic controllers, and moments later she could feel the pressure changing as the plane began its slow descent toward Lakemont's airport.

As soon as the engines throbbed to a stop outside the terminal, Derek was out of his seat. He announced that he had arranged for a rental car and in an obvious afterthought asked Rachel if she needed a ride.

"No, thanks, I've got transportation." She watched him stride off toward the terminal, garment bag over his shoulder. "Don't I?" she murmured, looking at Colin.

He sounded curious. "Why wouldn't I give you a ride home?"

Rachel shrugged. "Because you think I owe you some explanations."

"Not *owe,* exactly, but..."

She swallowed hard. "I did some foolish things in Arizona, Colin," she began tentatively.

He tugged at a coppery curl. "Just give me a few minutes to get this baby tucked in for the night, and when we get to your place we'll talk about it, okay?"

When they entered the house, Bandit rose from his cozy nest in the cushioned rocking chair, stretched and yawned. Then he pawed at Rachel's knees until she sat down and hugged him close like a teddy bear. Colin leaned against the mantel and waited.

Rachel took a deep breath, and the words she'd been playing over in her head burst out. "I wasn't very high up in the ranks," she said. "Certainly not on a par with the vice president of student affairs. I knew Derek, of course, but there was such a difference in our levels that it wouldn't have been proper to date. At least that's what I thought at the time. Then, out of the blue, he started inviting me out. Gave me a real rush. For a while I was flattered. That was before I found out why he was dating me."

Her voice broke. Her eyes were stinging; she tried to blink the tears away, but without success.

Colin said something under his breath and moved to the couch to put his arms around her. Rachel struggled for a moment, but his encircling arms were so warm and sheltering and comforting that she gave up and relaxed against him.

"Go ahead and cry," he said.

Even in the midst of her tears Rachel couldn't help noticing how her head fit perfectly into the curve of his neck and how his arms lay so comfortably around her. It felt almost as if the two of them were adjacent pieces of a jigsaw puzzle. Her hand crept up the front of his shirt until her fingers lay gently across his collarbone. His heartbeat made a soothing rhythm against her palm.

"I'm glad you waited to do this," Colin murmured. "It wouldn't have been very comfortable in the plane—cockpits are worse than sports cars, you know."

Rachel laughed through her tears. "Is that why you keep that tank of yours? Because it's got so much room?"

"Don't make nasty remarks about my car." His fingertips brushed the velvety hollow of her cheek. "You've got the most magnificent skin. It doesn't even get blotchy when you cry."

"Good thing, too." Her voice caught.

Colin's arms tightened reassuringly. "Want to tell me the rest?"

"About the same time Derek started to notice me—" Rachel swallowed hard and had to force the words out "—I came into a little money."

She stopped, and finally Colin said, "After your mother died, you mean? Or did you embezzle it from the scholarship funds?"

Rachel blew her nose and smiled a little. "It was perfectly legal. You see, not very many people knew about it, and so I thought..."

"That Derek's timing was just coincidental."

"He knew, of course. But by the time I realized he knew..."

Colin groaned. "He'd managed to get a good deal of it away from you, I suppose? And when the money was gone, he no doubt vanished, too. Rachel, how can you believe I'd think less of you for something like that? It's no surprise."

Her eyes widened. "It isn't?" Her voice was little more than a gasp.

"Of course not. I already know you're a terror when it comes to spending money. If you had help, you'd be unstoppable."

Rachel bit her lip. "Colin—"

"It's all right," he whispered against her lips. "It's all right." And as he kissed her—slowly, sensually—she almost began to believe him.

Her mouth softened and opened under his, and very gently and leisurely he explored its depths. He kissed her for a long time, and when finally he turned his attention to the skin at her temple, Rachel murmured a half-conscious protest.

Colin whispered, "I know. I don't want to stop, either. That's why I'd better go right now, before we both lose our heads."

Rachel felt as if she'd slammed into a wall. Her face flamed so wildly she could actually feel the heat radiating from her cheeks. "And do something we'll really regret?" Her voice was sharp. "I hardly think that's likely."

"As a matter of fact," Colin mused, "you might be right. I suspect I wouldn't regret it a bit."

She glared at him. His eyes were full of wicked humor.

"And I don't think you'd regret it, either," he whispered. He kissed the point of her chin, and then he was gone.

SHE RAN INTO DEREK on Monday, as he was having lunch with Ted Lehmann in the student union. She saw them as she was waiting in line for a table, and she would have left if Dawn hadn't been with her. And as luck would have it, the table right next to the president's was the one that opened up for them. Fortunately, however, just as Rachel and Dawn arrived, Ted and Derek stood up to leave. Spotting Rachel, the president said, "Allow me to introduce you to Derek Hamilton. He's interviewing for—"

Derek's eyes narrowed. "Then you didn't send her down to meet me, Dr. Lehmann?"

The older man's brow furrowed. Rachel thought his expression might be distaste at being interrupted. But his voice was level. "You went with Colin, after all, Rachel? I hope you had a good weekend."

From the corner of her eye, Rachel saw Derek's jaw tighten. Now he knows, she thought. "The trip was very enjoyable, Ted," she said. "But we just went down for the day to take in a musical."

Derek laughed harshly. "Why not the art museum and the ballet? I'll bet he really would have enjoyed that—if he understood any of it."

Rachel pretended not to hear. She took the chair that let her keep her back to him and picked up her menu.

Dawn watched as the men left the dining room. "What was that all about? You didn't seem impressed. Personally, I thought he looked like a good addition to the environment."

Rachel didn't look up from the list of sandwiches. "If you're lucky, you won't have to put that judgment to the test."

"What was that?"

"Never mind, it wasn't important. I'm having a Reuben, I think. What about you?"

Dawn ignored the distraction. "I hoped this little fling with Crash McKenna might help you get over your dislike of men, Rachel."

"I never said I dislike men in general. I just said I didn't intend to acquire one of my own."

Dawn smiled mischievously. "You don't? Then what do you call Crash? Just another house pet?" Before Rachel could retort, she had breezed on to another subject. "What are you wearing to the dance Saturday?"

"Dance? I didn't know there was one."

"It's Fall Festival, Rachel."

"I'm aware of that. But I thought the festival was just the football game and the street fair."

"What sort of party would it be without a dance? Shall we go shopping after work and find you a dress?"

"Oh . . . no, I don't think so."

"Why not?" Suspicion crept into Dawn's voice. "You haven't broken up with him, have you? Oh, dear, I'm so sorry for teasing you."

"No, Dawn. I haven't broken up with him." And when Thanksgiving comes, Rachel thought, the sympathy is going to be unbearable. Why hadn't she thought about that before? "I'm not going shopping because I already have a dress I can wear for the dance."

Dawn started to laugh. "That is the most transparent excuse I've ever heard for going straight home every night just in case he drops by!"

Rachel opened her mouth to deny it, and then decided that protesting would only give Dawn a reason for more hilarity. She was certainly not staying home because Colin might drop by. What Dawn wanted to believe didn't matter.

Nevertheless, when there was a knock on her kitchen door that evening, her throat tightened and her heart leapt. Telling herself not to be ridiculous, she turned down the burner under her pot of marinara sauce and answered the door.

Colin dropped a kiss on the tip of her nose and brushed past her to set a big brown paper bag on the tiny kitchen table. "Two things," he said briskly. "First, did you know you have a horde of urchins crawling all over your property?"

She was standing stock-still in the middle of the room with the now-forgotten stirring spoon still in her hand. "Yes. The neighborhood kids are picking up all the loose branches."

"Ah, that explains it. You're paying them by the branch obviously."

"Well, sort of," Rachel admitted. "The more they pick up, the better the pay. How did you know that?"

"Because they're now up in the trees breaking off limbs. Shall I go throw them out bodily?"

"No. Just tell them it's time to quit."

He started out the door and Rachel called after him, "Didn't you say there were two things you wanted to tell me?"

Colin turned. "Yes. The second one is you're dripping something all over the floor. What is that stuff, anyway?"

Rachel looked down at the puddle of marinara sauce at her feet and sighed.

By the time she'd cleaned up the mess, Colin had rounded up the half-dozen or so children and had them lined up in a neat row on the tiny side porch. When Rachel came to the door, the oldest of them said meekly, "We're awfully sorry about hurting the trees, Miss Todd."

She shot a look at Colin.

He prompted the child. "And?"

"And we don't think you should have to pay us at all, since we didn't do our job right."

Rachel studied the downcast little faces. "I'm sure that next time you'll come and ask me if you're not certain exactly what to do," she said, and they all nodded. She pulled a handful of dollar bills out of her apron pocket and passed them out down the line.

"You're a soft touch, Rachel Todd," Colin accused as he followed her into the kitchen. "The little monsters should have been whipped, not paid."

"You handle neighborhood relations in your way, I'll take care of them in mine." She picked up her spoon again. The sauce was starting to thicken nicely. "What's in the bag?"

"Would you believe Chinese food?"

"Not in my kitchen. There's a picnic table in the park just down the street."

"That's the kind of heartless thing I thought you'd say. Fortunately it's not Chinese food. It's a present."

"I thought we agreed to share expenses, Colin, and there's no room in this arrangement for gifts."

"I let you buy the tickets, didn't I?" He added in a murmur, "Only because I was afraid to ask how much they cost, but of course that's beside the point."

"Colin..." Her voice held a warning note.

"But books and candy and flowers are allowed by the rules of etiquette. You said that yourself." He pulled a thick paperback out of the bag and handed it to her. "So here's a book. And the rest of this isn't a present for you, it's for Bandit."

Rachel looked at the book cover, which featured a cardinal in full brilliant red plumage. "A bird identification guide? Why?"

He tugged gently at the gold nugget at her throat and said, as if the answer was obvious to anyone with half a brain, "Because Bandit can't read, so you'll have to look up the identifications for him." He pulled a flat box out of the bag. "Where can I find a screwdriver?"

Rachel looked at the box with apprehension. "Bottom drawer beside the sink. But..."

He dug out the tool, opened the box, and spread what looked like a hundred pieces of glass and redwood on the table. Within a couple of minutes, his project had begun to take shape.

A bird feeder, Rachel thought with a sigh. Just what I need.

But Colin, whistling as he worked, seemed to be enjoying himself. "This will entertain the cat while you're gone," he said. "We'll put it up outside the living-room window, and he can lie there on the ledge and sun himself all day and drool over the birds."

Rachel decided she might as well play along. "You're sure the frustration of not being able to hunt them won't drive him into a depression? I wouldn't know where to start looking for a cat psychiatrist."

"Don't worry. This will be a whole lot better for his brain than watching television." He slid a piece of glass into place. "You could have gone to Chicago with me again tonight."

"Flying Derek back to O'Hare? No, thanks."

"I thought that's what you'd say."

Rachel let the silence drag out. Finally she said tentatively, "He didn't stay long."

Colin shrugged. "Meaning that his interview didn't take enough time for him to be a serious contender for the job? I wouldn't know about that."

"But if you're back already, you must have left—"

"I didn't go."

"What?"

"I told Ted that Derek could walk to Chicago for all I cared."

"Colin! You didn't!"

"It's the first time in almost six years I've refused to do anything Ted asked. I do have some standards."

Rachel's heart seemed to be stuck between her vocal cords. "What did Ted say?"

"He didn't fire me, if that's what you mean." He sniffed appreciatively. "And in case you're worried, Rachel, your name didn't come up at all."

She relaxed. She should have known that Colin would be gentleman enough to keep her out of it, even if Ted Lehmann had come straight out and asked. "Would you like to stay for dinner? It's spaghetti with marinara sauce, that's all."

He turned to give her a smile that made her insides flutter a little. "Sure, I'll stay. It smells awfully good for something that isn't Chinese."

She cooked the pasta while he finished assembling the feeder. He'd even brought a large plastic sack containing seeds of every size, shape and color, and a hook for the porch. By the time he came in from hanging the feeder, dusting his hands in satisfaction, she had cleared and set the table.

"I had a couple of reasons for coming today," he said.

Rachel was just setting a steaming plate in front of him. Her hand slipped and the china hit the table with a thud.

"This is your big weekend," Colin went on, "so I thought perhaps we'd better make our plans."

Rachel sat down across from him and shook out her napkin. "Good idea. I've already embarrassed myself by not knowing I had a date for a dance on Saturday night."

"Sorry. I assumed Dawn would already have filled you in on that sort of detail. Is there anyone else in particular you want to convince?"

She thought about it and shook her head. "My supervisor probably won't be anywhere around. She hasn't said a word about her nephew in days, anyway."

"Her nephew?"

"Yes. She was trying to fix me up with him. But the word must have gotten back to her, either from Dawn or my secretary, that I'm not unattached anymore."

"I told you if we were seen together a lot at first, people would get the message."

"Well, much as I hate to admit it, you were right. After the festival we can taper off and nobody will even notice."

"Don't forget about Thanksgiving."

"I couldn't possibly," Rachel said dryly. "It features in my dreams. What's a McKenna celebration like, anyway?"

"Oh, our philosophy is pretty much like the Pilgrims' when they started this whole tradition."

"Meaning what? You eat corn pudding and fish?"

He made a face.

"Well, they probably didn't have turkey at the first Thanksgiving, you know."

"I've always felt sorry for the poor souls, too. They had no idea what they were missing."

"So tell me about this philosophy."

"Oh, just as the Pilgrims did, we invite everyone we can think of, whether friend or foe, and party for as long as the food holds out."

"Oh, joy," Rachel said faintly.

Colin grinned. "You'll like it, I think. But back to this weekend and Fall Festival. The *Chronicle*, bless its corporate expense account, rented a box for the football game, and Anne invited us to come to the party."

"I don't know, Colin. Is it the whole family?"

"Not really. Mostly it's Garrett business associates. A dull crowd, if you ask me, but if the weather's not great it's a whole lot nicer to be inside a glass box." He twisted spaghetti around the tines of his fork and added casually, "Camryn won't be there—she's not climbing any more steps than she has to till after the baby arrives."

Rachel smiled ruefully. "She wasn't bad, really. She hardly said a word about us as a couple when you weren't around."

Colin frowned. "Honestly? In that case, I really am worried about what she's up to."

Even after the dishes were cleaned up, Colin seemed no more inclined than Rachel to move away from the safety of the kitchen, where the tiny table formed a barricade between them. In fact, it was Colin who proposed they play penny-ante poker.

The suggestion took Rachel by surprise, and it was a few minutes and a couple of hands later that she understood what he was up to. He was protecting himself from a repeat of the night before.

The realization annoyed her. Colin might have come dangerously close to losing his head, she admitted. She'd had a few crazy thoughts along that line herself. But last night had been emotionally bizarre, too, with her shock over Derek. It wasn't likely to happen again.

Still, she told herself, they did have another whole month to keep up the facade. And now that they knew there were dangers involved, it was only common sense to avoid them.

But after he left, she stared at herself in the mirror as she smoothed night cream onto her face and wondered whether he'd wanted to kiss her, after all.

CHAPTER SEVEN

RACHEL TESTED her iron for the fourth time and decided that it was still not hot enough to properly press the paisley cotton blouse she intended to wear to the football game. She turned the temperature up a bit and leaned against the mantel to finish her grilled-cheese sandwich while she waited. The opening kickoff wasn't for another couple of hours, she reminded herself, so she had plenty of time. No need to feel frazzled. After she was dressed, she could still tidy up the house before Colin arrived and probably have time left over to go through the week's mail.

On the wide ledge under the front window, Bandit sat up and lazily nudged the curtain aside with his chin.

"Checking to see if your feathered friends are still there?" Rachel asked. She saw the dark brown tail twitch as if in answer and caught a glimpse of movement on the front porch. Too big to be a bird, she thought with a groan, and reached the door just as Colin put his finger on the bell.

"I chased off two woodpeckers and a chickadee," he said. "Accidentally, of course. It looks as if the feeder has gotten quite the reputation already."

Rachel tipped her head back and looked up at him in mock disgust. "The little beggars are putting up billboards all over town, I'm convinced of it. 'All You Can Eat, Rachel's Feeding Station, Waukegan Street.'"

Colin grinned. "You've had a few birds, then?"

"Thousands. The gift of the feeder included a lifetime supply of seed, didn't it? They've already consumed the bag you brought."

"Well, I hadn't exactly—"

"Oh, I don't expect you to deliver it from now on," Rachel said airily. "Just let me know where to buy the stuff, and I'll charge it to you." Then she relented and added seriously, "The birds are beautiful. It was a very thoughtful gift, Colin."

"I'm glad you're enjoying it. Are the birds the reason you're still in your pajamas at one in the afternoon?"

Startled, Rachel glanced down at the dark green sweat suit she was wearing. "These are not pajamas."

"Oh? Does that mean at bedtime you prefer little lacy things with ruffles and ribbons?"

"Colin, that's really none of your business."

"I know, but I've never understood why it is that the questions I shouldn't ask are also the most fun. Are you going to be ready soon?"

"Why should I hurry? The game doesn't start for a while." She checked the iron again. It was too hot now, so she turned it down and began pressing a towel to dissipate the extra heat.

"There are other things to do in the meantime."

"Like ironing a blouse to wear," Rachel said. "I do need a little time for necessities now and then. Cleaning house is not something that can be put off forever."

He glanced around the room and shrugged. "It looks fine to me. Besides, I gave you all morning. What did you waste it on? Shopping?"

Rachel pursed her lips primly and tried to look innocent. So what if she'd decided at the last minute that the dress she had intended to wear to the dance wasn't appropriate, after all? Her sudden decision to get a new one had nothing to do with Colin.

He pounced on a shopping bag in the corner. "You did. Rachel, you're hopeless."

She set the iron down cautiously on the sleeve of her blouse. "I don't need to account for my time to you. Besides, you were here almost every evening last week. When am I supposed to do all this stuff?"

"I don't care, as long as it's not right now. Put your clothes on."

Rachel kept ironing. "I have to finish this blouse before I can wear it, Colin."

"Why? You're going to put a sweater over it, aren't you?"

"Yes."

"Then you only need to iron the collar and cuffs."

"What would your mother think of that trick?"

Colin smiled. "Where do you suppose I learned it?"

Rachel took her time. The blouse was tailored, but it had a lot of details that took careful attention. "What's so important, anyway?"

"You'll see. Dress warmly."

"Why? I thought you said we'd be in an enclosed box at the football game." She unplugged the iron, draped the blouse over her arm and went off toward her bedroom without waiting for an answer.

A few minutes later, Colin called, "At this rate, how are you ever going to find time to learn to fly?"

Rachel stopped brushing her hair and yelled back, "Do you want me to rush around and end up looking as if I was put together by a seamstress with a hangover?"

Colin didn't answer that. "Or have you changed your mind about taking lessons?"

Rachel was still fastening her earrings as she reappeared in the living room. "Maybe the whole idea was just a passing whim. The more I think about it, the less sense it makes."

"Flying?" He sounded insulted.

"For me," Rachel added quickly. "As a hobby, I mean."

Colin snorted. "The truth is, you've spent all your loose cash on clothes, haven't you? And after I let you win at poker, too. You ungrateful wench."

"You did not let me win! I beat you."

"A couple of hands, yes. You're not bad at bluffing. But the rest was no coincidence."

Rachel had stopped listening and was watching the cat. Bandit was hunkered down in the center of the carpet, his tail switching, obviously stalking something. "What's he after?"

Colin stooped to take a look. "An insect."

"In my house? Eek! Get rid of it, would you?"

"It's only a box-elder bug, Rachel. He won't hurt anything. They don't munch on wool sweaters or—"

"I don't care if he's a philanthropist. I hate bugs."

Colin picked up a slip of paper from her desk, coerced the insect onto it and removed him to the outdoors.

"I don't know what you think you've accomplished," Rachel pointed out when he returned. "One of the birds will probably get him within seconds."

"Ah, but that's the natural order of things. Stomping him into the carpet isn't. Anyway, you told me to get rid of him and I did. So, what changed your mind about flying?"

"Has anyone ever told you that you're downright stubborn, McKenna?"

"They've mentioned it. What happened?"

Rachel sighed. "I started thinking about the time it would take away from my job and the classes I'm going to be starting soon. Besides, if God had intended me to fly—"

Colin nodded in enthusiastic agreement. "—he'd have invented airplanes. I've said precisely the same thing, many times." He helped her into her coat and let his hands rest warmly on her shoulders, holding her against his body. "Rachel, our minds are tuned so perfectly together that—"

She swung the end of her scarf over her shoulder. The tassel hit Colin squarely in the mouth, and he had to stop talking in order to pick threads off his tongue.

"Blessed silence," Rachel murmured. "I'll have to make a note of how I managed it."

They were lucky enough to find a parking spot near the administration building. Rachel was startled to see the main street in front of the building roped off and lined for blocks with carnival rides, souvenir booths and food stands.

"It really *is* a street fair," she said.

"You wouldn't expect us to do anything halfway, would you?"

"Yes, considering this event must get canceled one year out of three because of snow."

"Oh, in those years it's even more fun," Colin assured her. "We all build forts on the commons and have snowball fights, and use the carillon tower for target practice. I hit the biggest bell once."

Rachel looked up at the four-story tower of the administration building. The bells were barely visible, and she couldn't imagine lobbing any object high enough to hit them. "With a snowball?"

Colin nodded. "It didn't hurt anything, but it made a terrible sound. Campus security was not amused. So, shall we start with cotton candy?"

It wasn't really a question, and before Rachel could voice an opinion, she found herself at a booth across the street in front of a glass case full of iridescent pink spun sugar. She watched with trepidation as the proprietor briskly rotated a long paper cone inside the case to gather an enormous serving.

While Colin paid for the treat, Rachel gingerly held the cone. "This stuff doesn't have the faintest resemblance to cotton," she objected, turning it back and forth for closer inspection. "In fact, it looks more like that pink insulation stuff they use in houses. So why is it called cotton candy?"

"Because it was invented before blown-glass insulation was. Besides, would you eat it if the name made it sound like something salvaged out of a derelict house?"

"*Me* eat it? I thought I was only holding it for you."

"We'll share." Colin caught her wrist and held the cone steady while he tore off an enormous hunk with his teeth. "You sound as if you've never tried it before," he added indistinctly.

Rachel eyed the confection. "I haven't."

"Never?"

He looked so astonished that Rachel wished she hadn't confessed. "Well, when I was a kid there was never any money for stuff like that."

"No carnivals? No Ferris-wheel rides? No shooting galleries?"

Rachel shook her head. "Not really. Those things weren't necessities, and if Mom had any spare cash we went to the movies, instead. It was more educational, she said."

"And of course when you grew up there was no time for silly stuff like carnivals. Well, my dear, you are going to have one of the best days of your life. Grab a bite of cotton candy for energy and we'll be off."

She tried it cautiously. The spun sugar felt gritty against her tongue for just an instant, and then it was gone, leaving only a sticky sensation behind. "What's the point?" she muttered.

Colin shrugged. "Keep at it. I guess it's an acquired taste."

They tried out every ride and pored over the souvenirs at every booth. Colin caught her studying a rack of stuffed toys and said, "Come on. I'll win one for you." He pulled her down the street to a shooting gallery and slapped his money down on the counter.

Rachel hung back a little. "Isn't this gambling?"

"Not for someone who's a decent shot."

"And you complain about how I spend my money," she grumbled. "It sounds to me as if you're the one who's throwing it away."

"Pick out your prize, my dear." He sighted the pellet gun, and the proprietor set the targets in motion.

Rachel sighed. "The big brown teddy bear."

Colin turned his head to stare at the stuffed animal. "All right," he said dubiously. "But you have to carry it."

Five minutes later, as they set off down the street, she was clutching the bear.

"You make a cute couple," Colin said. "His eyes are exactly the same color as yours."

"I'm charmed. And if I could find a way to hold on to him . . ." The bear wasn't heavy, but it was about the size of a two-year-old child, and every grip she tried soon became uncomfortable.

"What you need is a backpack to put him in. That would make everyone turn around and look."

"Exactly what I don't want." Finally she settled on carrying the bear balanced on her hip as if he were a baby.

Colin draped an arm around her shoulders. "I told you I'd win it."

"I could probably have bought it for what you dropped at the shooting gallery."

"But that wouldn't have been nearly as much fun, would it? And even if that's true, why are you grumbling about it, anyway?"

He sounded serious, and Rachel thought about it for quite a while before she shook her head in confusion. "I don't know, exactly. It just bothers me."

Colin's arm tightened. "Relax. I never gamble more than I can afford to lose."

She looked up at him. "In that case, it's not my concern, is it? Sorry, Colin. Thanks for the teddy bear."

"That's better." His fingertips began to massage her shoulder. Even through her thick coat, his touch felt good. "Of course, a kiss would be an even nicer way to tell me what you think."

"Here?"

Colin shrugged. "Why not? If anybody we know happens to see us, it will just add to the image. And in this crowd, anyone who doesn't know us won't pay any attention."

He was right about that, Rachel thought. In the midst of a busy carnival, they were safer—in a crazy kind of way—than if they'd been alone. Here, things couldn't get out of hand.

She looked up at him through her lashes. There was a curious light in his eyes, and she wondered what he was feeling. A little twinge of anticipation curled through her. All week he had hardly touched her.

And that, she told herself briskly, was a very good idea. What was she thinking about, anyway, to let herself get caught up in this performance?

She stepped away from him. "Isn't it time for the football game?"

Colin looked hurt. "Rachel Todd, you've got the most inconvenient memory I've ever run into," he complained.

"Well, you did say we were going, didn't you?"

"Of course, eventually. But I had no idea you were such a rabid football fan."

"I'm not. I—"

There was no mistake now about the expression in his eyes; pure wicked enjoyment was practically spilling out of him.

If he says another word, Rachel thought, I'll kick him!

He started to whistle, instead, a soft lilting melody she vaguely remembered from their evening at Brannigan's. He broke off only to say, "Look, there's a fortune-teller. Let's get our palms read."

"That's nonsense, Colin, and you know it."

"Of course it is. That's what makes it so much fun."

Whether the woman inside the dimly lit booth was really a fortune-teller or only volunteering for the day, she certainly looked the part. Her hair and face were almost hidden by bright scarves, and gaudy jewels dripped from her arms. Her voice was low and husky and hypnotic. She held Rachel's wrist and stroked the back of her hand, all the while staring into her eyes. Then she turned Rachel's hand over and drew her fingertips down across the palm.

"There is a dark man in your future," she droned.

"And in my present," Rachel pointed out. "He's right here in the tent now, as a matter of fact. That hardly qualifies as a prediction."

The fortune-teller ignored her and continued. "She's just getting warmed up," Colin whispered. "Give her a chance."

Rachel rolled her eyes.

By the time they left the tent, she was trying so hard to repress her giggles that she was almost choking. "She's got to be a volunteer raising money for the PTA or something," she gasped. "Telling you there's a trip in your future is like—"

"Of course she's a volunteer," Colin said. "Didn't you recognize her? That was your friend Dawn."

Rachel blinked. There *had* been something familiar about those eyes.

"Though I don't know," Colin went on. "She might have a gift, after all. She certainly pegged you straight when it came to finances. 'Watch out for matters of money,' she said, and we all know—"

"Are you certain she wasn't getting vibrations from you? Maybe she meant to warn you about hanging around shooting galleries." Rachel shifted the teddy bear into a more comfortable position. "It's a good thing this doesn't weigh what a child the same size would, or I'd be a cripple."

"Want me to help?"

"Would you?" Gratefully, Rachel held out the teddy bear. "I know I agreed to carry it, but . . ."

Colin wasn't paying attention; he was talking to a passing clown. A moment later he turned back to Rachel, holding a bright red helium balloon. He tied it ceremoniously to the bear's collar and gave the stuffed animal a pat on the back. "There you go. That will help take the weight off you, Rachel."

She glared at him. "That's what you call helping?"

Colin grinned. "A little extra lift never hurts." He took the bear out of her arms. "But I'll carry him over to the stadium. You understand, however, that I'm only doing this because I'm afraid your temper will snap and you'll abandon him like a baby on the orphanage steps."

"I don't care why you're doing it." Rachel flexed her arm in relief and then tucked her hand into the crook of his elbow.

They had missed the opening kickoff, but the game was still scoreless and the party in the newspaper's special box was just getting under way when they arrived at the top of the stadium.

Anne Garrett took one look at the bear and said, "Too bad the rest of the family isn't here, Colin. Camryn would get a real charge out of seeing you act so...so paternal."

"If she were here, I wouldn't be doing it." He settled the stuffed animal in a stadium chair and propped a Nicolet pennant in one fuzzy paw. Then he wrapped Rachel's scarf, which happened to be the home team's colors, around the bear's neck and stepped back to admire the effect.

Rachel was still chilled from the wind, which had picked up as they walked across the campus. She rubbed her upper arms in an effort to stop shivering. "Sometimes I think I should have gone to Florida, after all," she muttered.

Colin looked up. "That was your other choice? Well, I'm glad you came to Nicolet, instead."

It was a little thing, Rachel told herself, but still it made her feel warm and cozy. The very idea that he cared, that he would have missed knowing her.... She smiled at him, and only then did she see the mischief in his eyes.

"In Florida, the bug season lasts all year round," he added pleasantly. "You wouldn't like that at all, I'm sure."

Anne said, "Still, it can't be any worse than here. We have two seasons." She handed Rachel a mug of hot cider.

Rachel sipped it gratefully. "Two? I thought—"

"One is winter," Colin said. "The other is called road construction. It takes about nine months to repair all the potholes, and by then it's time for winter again."

A cheer went up from the first row of seats, followed almost instantaneously by a groan, and Rachel turned around to see what had happened down on the field.

In the front row of the box, Ted Lehmann patted the empty seat next to him, and Rachel moved down to sit in it. "You don't happen to have a pair of binoculars, do you?" he asked.

She shook her head and looked down at the field as the teams regrouped for the next play. "I see why you need them. I had no idea we'd be up so high."

He turned his gaze back to the game. "Sometimes, Rachel," he mused, "I have trouble seeing things even when they're right in front of my nose."

Rachel's breath caught in her throat.

He doesn't mean anything at all, she thought. It was the kind of careless statement anyone might throw out. Not every remark had a hidden message.

And yet, there was something different about the tone of Ted Lehmann's voice today, and the way he had looked at her, as if he knew...

I suppose I should have expected this, she thought. I should have anticipated that Derek wouldn't keep his mouth shut.

She didn't comment. There was nothing to say until she knew how Ted would handle his knowledge, and if he had hired Derek, after all. But surely he hadn't. Ted wasn't insensitive to nuances, and he had heard the nasty crack Derek had made about Colin.

"I hope you won't be disappointed," Ted said thoughtfully. "But I don't think I can hire Derek Hamilton."

"You don't?" Her voice was little more than a croak.

He turned to look at her. "We're like a family here at Nicolet. We stick together. We don't tell tales about each other."

He had not believed what Derek had said, then?

"And we respect each other's privacy," Ted went on gently. "I don't think the young man understands that sort of thing."

"Then..."

"What you do is your business, Rachel. Not mine, and not Nicolet's. But if you ever want to talk about it..."

Down on the field, Nicolet's quarterback unleashed a long pass, and the receiver made a perfect catch and headed downfield. All the Nicolet fans in the stadium were on their feet, screaming, before the touchdown was complete. By the time the cheering was over, Colin had pulled Rachel out of her seat for a hug of celebration, and half-a-dozen people had crowded between her and Ted Lehmann.

It was just as well, Rachel thought. They had said everything that mattered, anyway.

THE BALLROOM at the student union was crowded and very warm. As Rachel and Colin finished a dance and strolled back toward their table at the edge of the tiled floor, she fanned her face and said, "That last number was incredibly fast. I could stand a change of pace."

"So could I," Colin said. "It's stuffy in here, and the band's taking a break, anyway." He glanced at his watch. "Hey, it's almost midnight."

Rachel's eyes widened. "Already?" The evening couldn't be gone yet, she thought. She was enjoying it too much. "I suppose it's time to leave, then."

The corner of Colin's mouth quirked. "You sound like a child who's been sent to her room, Rachel."

She smiled ruefully. "If you're ready to go home . . ."

"Not exactly. How about a walk? Not far, just a block or two, to get some fresh air."

Rachel wrinkled her nose in distaste. Colin laughed and led her out to the checkroom to retrieve her fake-fur jacket. As they left the student union, he said abruptly, "Let's stroll over to the administration building."

"Why? There's no snow, so you can't build a fort or throw snowballs at the bells in the tower."

But despite her protest, she fell willingly into step beside him. Colin's fingers closed around hers, and he tucked their clasped hands into his coat pocket.

The wind had died down, and though the air was cold, it was not an unpleasant night for a walk. The fresh air felt good against Rachel's flushed cheeks.

On the sidewalk in front of the administration building, in the shadow of the bell tower, Colin stopped. He stood there quietly, still holding her hand inside his coat pocket, apparently looking at nothing. There was no glorious full moon and no dramatic display of stars. In fact, Rachel could see nothing at all that could possibly have captured his attention so completely.

She shifted from one foot to the other. "Well?" she prompted. "What's this all about?"

Above their heads, the bells stirred to life.

"It's a Nicolet tradition," Colin said as the first long stroke of midnight rang out. He slowly drew her hand out of his pocket and let it slip from his grasp. Then he turned her toward him, put both arms around her and kissed her.

For the first few moments, his mouth was cold against hers. Then, as the kiss softened and deepened, heat seemed to explode through Rachel's body. Within seconds she had ceased to notice the chilly air; they made their own little envelope of comfort. She released a tiny moan and burrowed against him.

He kissed her through the remaining eleven chimes of midnight, and by the time he was finished Rachel wasn't quite sure if the ringing in her ears was the echo of the bells or the pounding of her heart, reverberating through her head.

Colin raised his head. His hands slipped under the hem of her jacket and came to rest, warm and comforting and solid, at her waist, as if he knew that her legs had suddenly become less than reliable.

"I still don't quite understand," Rachel said. Her tone was huskier than usual. "You said...it's a tradition?"

"To be an official coed at Nicolet, a girl has to be kissed under the bell tower during Fall Festival." Colin's voice was a little slower than usual, as if he was having to concentrate on his words.

"I see." She leaned back in his arms, secure in the knowledge that he wouldn't let her slip, so she could look up at him more easily. "Then you're performing a public service in a sense."

He nodded slowly. "You could say that, I suppose. Not that I do this for just anybody, you understand," he added hastily.

She smiled. "One every festival, perhaps?"

"Rachel!" he sounded almost hurt. "A gentleman doesn't kiss and tell."

"Oh, I'm not interested in the numbers, exactly. I was just trying to figure out how you made the mistake."

Colin's brow furrowed. "What mistake?"

"I'm not a coed, you know," Rachel pointed out gently. "I'm in a different category altogether."

"You mean that new employees probably don't count, so I shouldn't have kissed you?"

"Something like that."

"Then what are we going to do about it?" He thought it over, and finally his face cleared. "I've got it. You'll just have to give the kiss back," he suggested softly, and his arms tightened ever so slightly around her.

The suggestion was so ridiculous that she laughed. Which was why, when he bent his head to kiss her the second time, her lips were parted and her breath was already doing funny things in her throat.

The first kiss had been fire, but the second held all the awesome power of a tidal wave. Colin's touch was just as gentle, yet this time Rachel had to hang on to him to keep herself from being swept away by the sheer overwhelming force of it. The sensation was strange, unlike anything she'd ever felt before. But she didn't feel threatened. In fact, she was almost like a sponge—thirstily absorbing him, greedily wanting to become a part of him.

She wasn't ready to let him go. For a moment after the kiss ended, she simply stood there in the circle of his arms, her fingers still digging into his shoulders as if he was the side of a mountain and her tenuous grip was the only thing keeping her from sliding off.

And that wasn't far wrong, she reflected.

Very dimly she was beginning to understand what was happening to her—why she'd been so delighted by the silliness of the day and why the evening had sped by as they danced. She had not given a thought to her friends or his family; she had simply enjoyed herself in Colin's company.

She had set out to create an illusion, and she had done it so well that now she found herself caught up in the illusion—and wishing it were reality.

CHAPTER EIGHT

I WOULDN'T MIND at all, Rachel thought, if he honestly saw me as beautiful and funny—and maybe as the woman he'd like to spend forever with.

The shock of that realization made her eyes widen into huge hazel pools. But it wasn't as if she expected—or even wanted—a declaration of love, she told herself hastily. It was far too soon for anything like that.

What she wanted was much simpler. If only what they were pretending could be the reality—two people enjoying themselves, getting to know and like each other, with no expectations for the future. Then, perhaps—someday—they might find that together they had something that was truly important.

Colin said uneasily, "Rachel, I'm sorry. I had no intention—"

She shook her head. "No. It's not you." She had to force the words out, for her voice hardly worked at all. But it was just as well that she couldn't say much. It was certainly not the time to go around blurting out foolish wishes, before she'd even had a chance to think!

She realized she was still clinging to him. She had to concentrate in order to loosen her grip on his shoulders, because what she really wanted to do was fling herself against him and ask for another demonstration of the Nicolet tradition.

The cold air hit her with a rush, as if some protective bubble had suddenly burst, and she started to shiver uncontrollably. Colin pulled the collar of her jacket up around her face and turned her toward the parking lot where they had left the car. "I think it's time to go home," he said.

Rachel nodded.

For once, he didn't have much to say, either. The silence in the car made Rachel uneasy. Yes, she admitted, that kiss had gone beyond the bounds. But surely Colin's withdrawal was out of proportion. Had the episode frightened him so much that he didn't even have a quip? Had her reactions terrified him? Had he perhaps realized what she was thinking and panicked?

She tried to tease him about his uncharacteristic silence. "Last time it was quiet, you started complaining about my giving you the silent treatment," she reminded him. Too late, she remembered what he'd said he would do the next time she tried it, and her face turned flame red. Did he think she would consider carrying out that same threat? The very idea of kissing him again made her shiver.

Even that possibility did not bring the gleam of mischief back into his eyes. "I don't know what to say," he admitted. "I didn't intend that to happen, Rachel."

Obviously he'd meant the embrace under the bell tower to be exactly what the tradition dictated—a pleasant little kiss of welcome for a woman new to the campus. Sadness stabbed at Rachel's heart, but she fought the feeling. Of course that was what he had intended. She should have expected nothing else. He'd always made clear his feelings and his intentions. He had no wish to be tied down; that was, after all, the only reason he had agreed to get involved in her crazy scheme in the first place.

"I know," she said softly. "It's all right."

"Maybe we need to talk about this, Rachel." He cleared his throat uneasily. "When we've had a chance to think."

Rachel shrugged. His obvious discomfort made her uneasy, too. That was not a talk she'd enjoy, she was sure of it. Listening to him explain that he had really meant nothing by that silly kiss at all, and if she had misunderstood of course he was sorry, but . . .

No, she decided. There was no need to go into details. "There's nothing to talk about, really. It doesn't matter. A pleasant little kiss went astray, that's all."

He didn't answer for another block, until the car was safely in her driveway. "Yes. I suppose you're right."

Was that relief she heard in his voice? "Of course I'm right," she said.

He left the engine running. "I won't come in. I think it's . . . safer that way." He came around the car to help her out.

She closed her eyes for an instant to compose herself, and by the time he opened her door she managed to give him a playful smile. "That's probably a good idea. You're dangerous in close quarters, you know."

He stepped back. The timing was purely coincidental, Rachel told herself. He had to move out of the way for her to reach the sidewalk. But she couldn't help but wonder if he had stepped aside so quickly to avoid any possibility of her throwing herself into his arms.

The very idea annoyed her. But it also made her sad, and she groped for a way to put him at ease, to reassure him that she didn't expect anything more. With tremendous effort, she kept her voice light. "You really should watch yourself, Colin." She shook a teasing finger at him. "If you keep going around kissing people like that, someday some woman will lose her head and take you seriously."

He didn't seem to see the humor. "You could trigger a few forest fires yourself. Matches not needed."

Did he really think that? Rachel wondered. Or was he just trying to make it extra clear that what had occurred between them under the bell tower had been only the magic of the evening and didn't mean that the two of them were anything special?

"Maybe it's a good thing Fall Festival comes only once a year," she said.

He stood beside the car while she walked to the house. She was glad he was gentleman enough to wait until she was safely inside. Yet another part of her wished he'd driven off immediately. In the glare of the headlights, she felt as if she was on a stage or a modeling runway, with every step being critically observed, and suddenly she was aware of her body in ways she'd never been before.

She had not known, for instance, that her natural walk could set a dress swaying like the hoop skirt of a Southern belle. Would Colin think she was purposefully doing that to impress him?

She breathed a sigh of relief when she reached the door—and froze an instant later with her key already in the lock as he called her name.

Was there a different tone in his voice? Pain, perhaps? Uncertainty?

She heard the car door slam and his step crunching in the leaves on the drive, and her hand tightened on the key. Was he coming after her to say he wanted to change the ground rules, after all?

Don't dream like that, she warned herself. It's only going to hurt worse if you do. And sure enough, when she turned toward him she saw that he was carrying the bear he had won for her that afternoon at the shooting gallery.

"We forgot the poor guy after the football game," Colin said. "He's been sitting in the back seat getting colder ever since."

Rachel pushed the door open and reached for the animal. It was chilly against her fingers, and when her hand brushed Colin's the contrast was so extreme she pulled back as if she'd been burned.

That wasn't very nice of me, she thought. But she didn't know how to explain that the reaction had been involuntary, not a way to avoid his touch. Instead, she said without looking up, "Thank you for a beautiful day, Colin. And a memorable Fall Festival."

He nodded. "Maybe I'll stop by tomorrow, if that's all right."

Rachel nodded, and she watched him go before she went inside. She did not turn on the lights, and she did not bother to hang up her coat. She just sank down in her favorite chair. Bandit came to sit on her lap, and she hugged him close, heedless of the loose fawn-colored hairs that seemed magnetically attracted to the nubby fabric of her new dress.

"You're a dimwit, Rachel Todd," she said. "On a colossal scale." The words seemed to ring through the quiet house as powerfully as the bells of midnight had reverberated through her bones.

The problem she faced was plain and simple. She had not wanted to take the chance of getting close to any man ever again, so she had set up this incredible scheme. Now it had backfired, and she was caught in her own foolish masquerade. She had fallen for Colin Mc-Kenna—

She stopped herself right there. "That's silly," she muttered. "Of course I find him attractive. There'd be something wrong with me if I didn't. But I'm not in love with him, or anything close to it. I simply like him a lot, and under ordinary circumstances—" she took a deep breath "—if I let myself, I could fall in love with him."

But of course, ordinary circumstances did not apply in this case, where every gesture either of them had made was no more than playacting. And if she let herself believe that anything that had happened between them had been real, she'd be setting herself up for a truly devastating blow when this show of theirs came to the end of its run.

But it has been real for me, Rachel realized. I haven't been playing a part.

At first, perhaps, she'd only been performing the role expected of her. But then, before she'd even realized it, affection for the man had crept up on her, and soon she wasn't performing at all, but acting as any normal woman would when in the company of a man she liked. It had felt very natural to laugh with him, to hold his hand, to share his activities, to kiss him... There had been no need to pretend, and so she had simply done what seemed right.

Was it possible that the same was true of Colin?

Had he sat through that whole play in Chicago holding her hand only because it was part of his personal script? But if that was why he'd done it, then it made no sense. Who'd have been likely to see them in a darkened theater more than a hundred miles from home?

And over the past few weeks, he had kissed her even when no one else could possibly have seen. In fact, now that she stopped to think about it, he seemed to have kissed her *especially* when no one else could have seen and been impressed by their supposed feelings for each other.

But did that indicate a change in his attitude, or only a desire to live the part so thoroughly that when they were in public their actions would look absolutely realistic to outsiders?

Was it possible that his feelings, too, had undergone a transformation? If Rachel had found herself suffering from a change of heart, couldn't the same thing have happened to Colin?

"Don't be such a dreamer," she told herself.

Still, that could explain the odd uneasiness she had sensed in him tonight; it could be confusion about how he really felt. That theory, she told herself stubbornly, made every bit as much sense as believing that he was concerned and full of regret over that fierce and passionate kiss for fear he'd misled her. It would even explain his saying that they had to talk about what had happened—and then putting it off. Perhaps it was because he honestly didn't know what he wanted to say.

Tomorrow, she thought. I'll see him tomorrow. By then he'll have thought it through.

She reminded herself that he had said "maybe." What if he didn't come?

Panic curled upward from the pit of her stomach. She fought it down by telling herself firmly that nothing had to be decided just now. Indeed, she didn't want to have choices forced upon her at this moment. All she really longed for was a chance for both of them to think it through and to find out if all this could possibly be real.

And with Thanksgiving Day still weeks away, there was plenty of time, wasn't there?

SUNDAY PASSED with agonizing slowness. Rachel couldn't settle to any task; her mind kept skittering off in odd directions. She scolded herself for acting like an adolescent with a crush, but whenever she heard a noise outside she jumped up to see if it was Colin.

By midafternoon she realized he probably wasn't coming. She forced herself to sit at her desk, partly because her bills and bookkeeping honestly needed attention, but mostly as discipline for her wandering mind. As long as she was working on her finances, she didn't dare let herself think of anything but numbers.

The philosophy worked so well that when Colin rang the bell an hour later, she actually wondered for an instant who it might be. Then she leapt up so fast she knocked a stack of bills off the corner of the desk.

He was leaning against the door frame, arms folded negligently across the front of a corduroy sports jacket. "Want to go to Brannigan's with me?"

"Sure." She saw a gleam of humor spring to life in his eyes and decided that a bit of hesitation might have served her better. She added, "You'll have to give me a few minutes, though."

His gaze slid lazily down her body, across her bulky cream-colored sweater and trimly tailored forest-green trousers. "To change clothes, I suppose? You look fine just the way you are."

There was a note of lazy appreciation in his voice, and Rachel colored a little. Trust Colin to notice that she was better dressed than she usually was for lounging around the house. She might as well have hung a sign around her neck announcing that she was waiting for him!

"You did say you might drop in," she said crisply. "Frankly, I thought you'd turn up this morning and expect me to be ready for another family dinner."

"Would I take you for granted like that?" He sounded honestly surprised. "Besides, Mother and Dad went off for a long weekend." He followed her across the living room.

"Where did they go?" Rachel picked up her fountain pen.

"Hard to say. It was supposed to be New Orleans, but Mother picked up the tickets, so they may have ended up in Hawaii, instead. What are you so busy with, anyway?"

"Bills." She stooped to gather the envelopes she had knocked onto the carpet. "You've been hanging around so much that I've been neglecting this kind of thing, and I can't put it off any longer."

"We wouldn't want a collection agency to repossess you, that's for sure." He helped to pick up the mess, then pulled a white handkerchief out of his pocket and began snapping it gently at the cat. "Do you mind if I get him a straw to play with while we're gone?"

Rachel shrugged. "You know where they are." She signed a check, tore it out and studied it before slipping it into the envelope. Her signature looked a bit shaky, she noticed, and her fingers were trembling just a little.

How perfectly ridiculous. Surely she wasn't so silly that she was going to feel awkward now whenever he was around!

She sorted through the stack of mail and wrote checks for half a dozen more bills before quitting. Colin was teasing Bandit with a bright pink soda straw, tossing and retrieving it. The man was more restless than usual today, she thought. He couldn't seem to sit still.

She licked the last stamp and said, "The rest can wait till next weekend, I suppose."

Colin tossed the straw once more and glanced at the pile of envelopes. "If you need to mail those, we can detour past the post office."

"Thanks, but I'm not that close to the deadline."

He grinned. "Oh? I thought you said you couldn't put them off any longer."

Caught in your own story, my girl, Rachel told herself. You'd better watch your step.

At Brannigan's the trio was already playing. Business was booming; they waited by the bar for a table to open up. Even the bartenders were busy today, and just as Colin ordered their drinks, Rachel tugged at his sleeve. "There's a booth," she said.

Peggy was passing by with a tray of empty glasses. "Grab it," she said. "I'll bring your drinks over."

They had to weave through the crowd, and finally Rachel sank into the booth with an air of triumph. "I feel as if I've won a prize." She laughed and unthinkingly reached out to touch Colin's arm.

His fingers closed around hers, warm and strong, and he smiled. She looked into his eyes and something deep inside her twisted. The sensation was not exactly painful, but it took her breath away as surely as if she'd been stabbed.

She'd looked at him hundreds of times in the past few weeks, and she'd always thought him handsome. But this was different. This time she didn't see dark hair, blue eyes, white teeth. She didn't even see the funny little crinkles at the corners of his eyes, or the creases around his mouth that came from laughing often and heartily.

This time, she looked across the table at him and saw the dear familiar face of the man she loved.

You fool, she told herself. You didn't even recognize what's happened to you. Last night she had constructed a sweet little scenario that someday, maybe, she and Colin would fall in love. But she had overlooked one very large truth—for her, ''someday'' and ''maybe'' no longer applied.

She didn't know how long she'd loved him. She supposed it didn't matter. It might even have happened that very first night in the rain, when he'd listened to her absolutely insane plan and not laughed himself into a fit. Or the night she'd told him about Derek, and he'd held her tenderly and mopped her tears.

''Colin...'' she began. But the ache in her throat kept her voice almost too soft to hear, with the music in the background.

I can't say it here, she thought. She couldn't tell him, in the middle of this busy noisy place, that she loved him. Colin would probably tip over the table and run. But she could—she *must*—tell him the rest. The other things that needed to be shared....

Peggy set an Irish coffee down in front of her. ''I got my letter from the admissions office yesterday, Miss Todd. It's all set up.''

Don't talk about it now, Peggy, Rachel wanted to say. But there was a subdued glow about Peggy as if someone had lit a candle deep inside her, and Rachel didn't have the heart to extinguish it. She put a hand gently on Peggy's wrist. ''That's great. I'm glad everything is working out so well for you.''

''What's happening, Peggy?'' Colin asked.

Peggy set a glass of ice in front of him and poured his ginger ale. ''I'm going to Nicolet, starting in January.''

Colin's eyebrows shot up. ''How are you going to manage that?''

Peggy grinned. ''Miss Todd fixed it up.''

Colin raised his glass in salute. "Miss Todd really is a miracle worker," he murmured.

Peggy nodded. "She got me a full scholarship, and a housing allowance and even money for books. I can give up my job at the ice-cream parlor and just work here on weekends for my spending money. I can hardly think about it without starting to cry. See what I mean? Here I go again." She made a face as she dashed moisture from the corners of her eyes. "You're awfully special, Miss Todd, and I hope Colin appreciates—"

A call from another table made her break off with an apologetic smile and hurry away.

Rachel looked down at the table in embarrassment. "Yes, Miss Todd," Colin said. "You're quite a miracle worker, in fact."

There was a dry note in his voice that made Rachel uncomfortable. She sipped her coffee and shrugged. "I'm just doing my job."

"You're awfully good at it, I'd say."

"I guess that's why they hired me."

Colin took a long swallow of ginger ale. "How long has Peggy been working on getting into Nicolet?"

There was no sense in trying to escape the question, Rachel thought. It would be too easy for him to check with Peggy. "A couple of weeks, I guess."

"Since she met you, in fact."

She nodded. "I suppose so."

The band took a break, and the noise level abruptly dropped. Colin didn't say a word for a long time. He simply stared at her.

Rachel toyed with her mug, sneaked a glance at him and finally said, "I wish you wouldn't look at me that way."

"Why? How am I looking at you?"

"As if you don't know me." She meant it to sound flippant, but it didn't come out that way.

"I'm beginning to think I don't. I'd have sworn Peggy had no dreams about Nicolet until you came along. Now suddenly it's all set."

"I'm sure Peggy doesn't tell you everything."

"Where did you find the money, Rachel? The—what was it again?—Carleton Fund?"

"As a matter of fact, yes. Peggy's exactly the sort of student the Carleton Fund looks for—dedicated, trying to make it on her own, but needing a little help."

"A little help?" he echoed dryly. "Full tuition plus living expenses?" Before Rachel had a chance to answer, he went on, "I'd like to know more about that fund."

"Sorry. It's an anonymous source, very confidential." The words came automatically; she had said them a hundred times before. "If I told where the money came from, that would be the end of the funds. The donor is a very private person, and—"

"Oh, I have no doubt of that." He leaned forward and put both elbows on the table. "Want to hear what I think?"

No, she almost said. But that was hardly a normal reaction. She shrugged. "Why not? Everyone's got a right to an opinion."

"I think *you're* the anonymous source."

Under the table, Rachel's nails cut into the palm of her hand. "Come on, Colin, you're always giving me grief about how I can't hang on to money—" She stopped. She needed a minute to think before she got herself in even deeper.

He didn't give it to her. "Precisely. You look like a very foolish spender. Take that fur coat, for instance."

"It's fake."

"I don't doubt it. You're not the sort who would wear mink even if it was a bargain. You like animals too much. But your coat is a damned good fake, and those things aren't cheap, either." He leaned back in his chair and said thoughtfully, "You don't ring true, Rachel. You haven't all along. You've got a nice car—not exotic, not attention-getting—but certainly not inexpensive. Your clothes aren't flashy, but they're top quality—they don't come from discount houses. That gold nugget you wear..." He put a finger out to touch it.

Rachel pulled back. "I told you where the gold came from."

"But it's the workmanship that costs in things like that, isn't it? And I bet that musical we saw wasn't the first time you've bought the best seats in the house."

Rachel bit her lip.

"I don't know exactly what Nicolet pays you," Colin mused, "but I could make a pretty good guess. On your salary, the only way to have all those things is to use plastic money and hope to pay it off someday."

"So?"

"So you're not just scraping by on your regular pay, are you? I saw the size of the check you were writing today to pay your credit-card bill. It didn't really register at the time, but I saw it."

Rachel felt as if the floor had shifted and was sliding out from under her. She'd been further off balance this afternoon than she'd realized, to be so careless.

"And I saw the name on your checkbook, too. Rachel C. Todd. What's the C stand for?"

"Catherine," she said coolly.

"Then I'll bet the 'Carleton' is a generation back. Your mother's name, maybe." He paused, then added quietly, "I can find out, you know. It's handy having a sister who sits in the publisher's office of a major newspaper. All she has to do is give the word, and there will be three reporters tracing every transaction you've ever made, Rachel C. Todd—"

"Don't, Colin. Please. It's certainly no crime, what I'm doing." She was trembling and fighting back tears.

"You've got some fancy explaining to do." His voice held a cold edge. "You said you came into a 'little' money—your mother's life insurance, I believe?"

Blindly, she defended herself. "I didn't say what it was. You assumed that."

"But you didn't correct me. You also didn't specify how much it was."

He knew it all, she thought, or at least enough that the details would make no difference. How had she ever let herself underestimate him so? She remembered thinking he was dangerous, but even then she hadn't had enough common sense to pull away before it was too late.

"No," she said quietly. "I didn't correct you. Because..." Her voice failed her. She fumbled for a tissue and blew her nose. Then she raised her chin and said, "Because I have so much money I can't even begin to tell you where it all is."

Colin didn't say a word, but his gaze, dark and steady, was fixed unblinkingly on her face. If there was a gleam of avariciousness in his soul, she thought, he did a good job of hiding it.

The cold edge was gone from his voice. In fact, he sounded almost gentle. "Where did it come from, Rachel?"

"Well, I didn't rob a bank," she said tartly. "And I didn't win the lottery, either. I inherited it from my father."

"The chemistry professor?" He was obviously startled.

Rachel nodded. "He didn't save it up out of his salary, obviously. He created a chemical process—it's too complicated to explain. It's even too complicated to understand, as far as that goes—I'm not scientific enough to comprehend it. But it's something they do with paint on cars that almost eliminates rust."

Colin didn't say anything, and his silence encouraged Rachel a little. "After my mother died, you see, I went to Arizona, because I knew that's where my father was. I was suddenly all alone, and I just wanted to be closer to him." She paused. "I didn't know anything about the money. It wasn't till after he died that I even knew about the patent and the royalties."

When she took a deep breath to tell him the rest, Colin said coolly, "And then all of a sudden you were a rich little girl, so you started thinking you were better than anyone else."

Rachel's eyes widened in shock. "I don't think that! Not at all!"

"This is what you were afraid Derek Hamilton would tell me, wasn't it?" He sounded almost bitter. "You are one twisted-up lady, Rachel Todd, hiding out and lying to protect your money!"

"Thank you very much, Colin," she snapped. "But you are not my psychotherapist!"

"No, I'm your stooge," he said. "You've been having a hell of a good time with this whole affair, haven't you?"

The accusation hit her with the force of a falling boulder, and Rachel struck back. "You're the one who made all the assumptions, Colin. I didn't tell you the money was gone. I didn't tell you Derek broke up with me, instead of the other way around. You assumed those things."

"You certainly didn't make any effort to tell the truth."

"As I remember, you didn't give me much of a chance. You were so certain you had everything figured out."

"I thought we were getting to be friends," Colin said. His voice was low and harsh. "But friends tell the truth, Rachel, even when it hurts." He stood up and thrust his arms into his leather jacket.

Rachel stared at her Irish coffee. "Are you going to take me home?" she asked meekly.

He had already turned away. He wheeled to face her, jaw tight, eyes fierce. "I don't leave a lady stranded," he said.

Rachel closed her eyes in relief. He would calm down on the drive, she thought. She would ask him in, explain. . . .

He tugged his money clip from his pocket, pulled out a bill, and dropped it on the table in front of her.

"Here," he said. "Take a cab."

He pushed his way through the crowd and was gone.

CHAPTER NINE

HE WAS RIGHT, of course, Rachel found herself thinking. She should have told him the truth from the beginning.

"Wait a minute," she said under her breath. How was she to have guessed when this little adventure first started that it would come to matter whether or not he knew about the money?

It certainly hadn't been important at first. What they were doing was only playacting; there was no reason to discuss the details of their lives. She hadn't asked Colin for a rundown of his past and a personal financial statement, and he had no right to demand such particulars from her, either. If their little scheme had gone off as originally intended, the question never would have come up. But it hadn't worked out that way.

Because of her growing love for Colin, Rachel had failed to keep a little distance between them as she had intended. That love had been so subconscious that she had not even admitted to herself that she hoped to build something permanent between them, and so she had not allowed herself to think about whether she owed Colin the truth.

And of course by the time she saw what she had done and knew how important this relationship was to her, she had let too many opportunities pass. There had been too many time she could have explained and hadn't.

Face it, Rachel, she told herself. You don't have to use words to tell lies. You did lie to him, by saying nothing at all.

No wonder he'd blown up at her, she thought. How was he to know that she'd actually been about to confide in him at the very moment Peggy came up to the table with her news?

Your timing stinks, Rachel.

She rubbed her temples in a futile effort to wipe out the pain hovering there. If she'd been able to tell him then, if Peggy hadn't interrupted, would it have made a difference? At least the information would have been voluntary, not forced out of her by circumstances. But maybe it would have already been too late for the truth.

I thought we were getting to be friends, he'd said, *and friends tell each other the truth.*

But friends listen, too, she reminded herself bitterly. Friends had time for explanations, and friends gave each other the benefit of the doubt. Colin had done none of that. Instead, he'd acted like a wounded bear because she hadn't confided in him. He'd acted like judge and jury, assuming he knew her motives—and dismissing them as inadequate—without any effort to understand why she didn't trust her secret to every person who happened along.

Peggy came by and scooped up the empty ginger-ale can. "Another Irish coffee, Miss Todd?"

"No, thanks. I'm leaving."

Peggy's eyebrows shot up. "Alone? Where did Colin go?"

"Away," Rachel said crisply.

"You had a fight, hmm? Gee, I hope I didn't cause it."

Rachel looked up in surprise. Was the woman psychic?

"Telling him he ought to appreciate you," Peggy elaborated. "Maybe I shouldn't have said it, even though it's true. Guys are funny that way."

"It wasn't your fault, Peggy." Rachel left Colin's twenty-dollar bill on the table. If she picked it up, she would probably tear it into shreds and mail it back to him. If she left it as a tip for Peggy, at least it would do some good.

"And he talks about me throwing money around," she muttered. She shrugged into her coat and went to call a cab.

Money! It had caused her a raft of problems, that was certain. Derek, of course, had been chief among them. But he hadn't been the only man to find Rachel much more fascinating after he knew about her money. Couldn't Colin even see that she had good reason to be wary of saying too much?

Perhaps it was just as well she hadn't tried to explain it all to him. Obviously it would have done no good. Colin was so shortsighted he probably thought she should have taken out an ad in the *Chronicle* to announce her good fortune and trusted that everyone she ran into would have only her best interests at heart!

The cabbie tried to start a conversation on the way across town. Rachel answered in monosyllables. Her mind was still racing in circles and coming to the same conclusion—she had done the only thing she could at the time. She could not have been expected to know from the beginning that this incredible game might be important, after all, or that Colin would turn out to be different from Derek.

In fact, Rachel reminded herself, there was no actual proof of that even yet—except for the whisperings of her heart, which said that of course Colin wasn't like Derek. He could never be so cold and calculating and out to improve his own lot.

Still, her heart wasn't known for being reliable, she reminded herself bitterly. She had believed Derek for a long time, even after the evidence had started to pile up. And as for Colin, well, on the night of Anne's dinner party when he'd told Rachel that his sister had married the Lakemont *Chronicle,* he had sounded quite calm about it and seemed to think it had been the sensible thing to do.

Of course it was sensible, Rachel told herself, because Anne was obviously deeply in love with that handsome husband of hers. And Colin had only been joking.

Finally the cab stopped in front of her house. Rachel paid the bill and went inside. She did not turn on the lights; the dim glow of the street lamps provided enough illumination to feed Bandit and make herself a cup of tea.

She carried her cup into the living room and settled down on the couch by the fireplace. The house felt chilly, and she found herself longing for a crackling little blaze to warm her feet. But she still hadn't had the chimney checked out for safety, and in any case, she didn't have the energy to build a fire.

Instead, she curled up and pulled a lightweight quilt around her shoulders, then put her head down against the fat fur tummy of the bear Colin had won for her at the street fair only yesterday. The feel of the soft fur against her cheek and the hint of Colin's scent that still clung to the bear should have comforted her. Instead, she felt more alone than ever.

The sudden sweep of loneliness shouldn't be so difficult to accept, she reminded herself. She was used to it. Even as a child, she'd always been a bit apart from other people, for Alice Carleton Todd had not encouraged her only child to make friends.

Rachel hadn't pushed the question. Even as a little girl, she'd sensed her mother was different. Other children's mothers laughed a lot and said silly things and played games. Alice Todd didn't. She had no time for frivolity.

As Rachel grew older, of course, she had come to understand that her mother was extraordinarily bitter over the blows life had dealt her. It didn't take a genius to see that it couldn't have been easy for Alice when Rachel's father had walked out of their lives, leaving her with no help, no money and a toddler to raise.

In the midst of her own adolescent rebellion, however, Rachel had found herself questioning what little she had been told about her father. Had he really been the villain Alice had painted him? Had Alice's coldness and lack of humor come about because of her husband's desertion, or had those things always been a part of her nature and therefore contributed to the breakup? Heaven knows, sometimes Rachel herself preferred that home was some other house. Had her father felt the same way and ultimately acted on his wish?

And more important yet—at least in Rachel's mind— was the question of why Henry Todd had not kept in contact with his daughter. Had he not *wanted* to stay in touch with Rachel, as Alice implied? Or had he been discouraged from writing or telephoning her? Was it possible that Alice had even intercepted letters or calls—told him that Rachel had no interest in him?

Rachel sat up, pushed the quilt aside and took a sip of her tea. It was lukewarm, but she hardly noticed. She was lost in the past, thinking about the spring almost four years ago when Alice Todd had died.

In the first few months afterward, Rachel had brooded over her loss, for despite the difficulties and the tensions between them, she had loved her mother and knew that Alice had cared deeply for her.

They had been alone together for a very long time. Rachel had no other family to turn to, and the sense that now she was completely alone in the world was almost as difficult to bear as the loss itself.

And so it was natural that she had found herself wondering, as the months went on, about her father—whether he would want to know about Alice's death and whether he would hold out his arms to Rachel and assure her she was not alone, after all.

That was why, after her initial grief had settled into acceptance, she had begun to look for Henry Todd.

She knew from the beginning that when she found him, she would not be able to just call him up and announce herself, or ring his doorbell without warning. For him, after more than twenty years, that sort of encounter would be almost like running headlong into a child long ago given up for adoption. Even if it was a pleasant surprise, it would be no less a shock.

And Rachel could not simply write him a letter, either. The man might have married again; there was certainly no reason he couldn't have. He might have a wife and a whole new family who were unaware of the existence of a daughter from a former marriage.

So, as she searched university catalogs and professional organizations, she planned her course of action. When she found Henry Todd teaching chemistry at a university in Arizona, she didn't telephone him. She didn't write. She sent out her résumés, instead, and when a small college near Henry's university offered to hire her, she packed what she could into her old car, put everything else up for sale and left the green forests of Michigan for the desert sands of the Southwest. She would find a way to scrape an acquaintance with him, and only then would she tell him who she was....

Restlessly Rachel wandered into the kitchen and put the kettle on again. She didn't want tea; she wanted to stop thinking. But there was no way to turn off her mind.

Damn you, Colin, she thought, for stirring all this up once more, when it was finished....

Those first few months in Arizona had been wonderful. Her job was more demanding than any she'd held before, but also more rewarding. There wasn't much time to spend in research on Henry Todd, though it took little effort to learn he was not married. He had a reputation among students, in fact, as a crusty and demanding old professor who lived for—and virtually in—his laboratory. That fact, sad as it was, was almost a comfort to Rachel. To shut himself off like that must mean he had a hidden side, a sorrow he tried not to show to the world—and what could that sadness be if it was not Rachel herself and his loss?

Still, she was unwilling to take the chance that a sudden shock might upset him. So she began looking for mutual acquaintances who could break the news gently. In the meantime, she was not unhappy or impatient. For one thing, free for the first time in her life of the watchful eye of her mother, she could make friends as she wished. And she could date when and whom she pleased.

She didn't date Derek Hamilton, though she was aware of him and admired him. She thought he was aware of her, too, but the gap between a vice president and a mere financial-aid counselor was too great. At least, that was how she'd explained it to herself when she got her promotion to assistant director and Derek had first asked her out.

But that had been later, of course, much later, after she'd finally met her father. After she knew about his life's work....

When the telephone rang, Rachel was so lost in thought that she didn't hear it at first. When she finally answered, Colin sounded hesitant. "Rachel?"

The rock that had been in the pit of her stomach since he'd left her at Brannigan's seemed to grow three sizes larger. "Who else did you expect?" She shifted her grip on the receiver. "Why are you calling, anyway? To check up on me?"

"I drove by. The lights weren't on. I was worried you hadn't gotten home yet."

"I'm a big girl. I can take care of myself."

There was a tiny silence. "I'm sorry. I shouldn't have walked out on you like that."

"Why? Have you had second thoughts about letting such a good opportunity slip away?"

His voice tightened. "I was worried, dammit! Oh, what's the use? Obviously I shouldn't have bothered you, so I won't keep—"

"Don't you hang up on me, Colin McKenna!" Rachel said fiercely. "I've got a few things to say to you. How dare you treat me as if I've committed a crime!"

He sounded startled. "Maybe if you weren't sneaking around acting as if you were—"

"It's my money, and what I do with it is no one's business but my own."

"Very true. Don't you understand that it's the principle of the thing that bothers me?"

"Meaning that I should have told you?" She shifted her grip on the telephone and rubbed her suddenly sweaty palm on the quilt. "Why, Colin? Who says I owe you an explanation of anything I choose to do?"

There was a long silence before he said, "You don't, of course." His voice was low and very flat. "Good night, Rachel. I won't disturb you again."

She put the telephone down and buried her face in the teddy bear's fat tummy. Two painfully hot tears seeped into the soft fur.

What on earth had she been hoping for when she flung that last question at him, she asked herself bitterly. That he would tell her she owed him the truth because he loved her?

What a fool she was even to let herself hope for anything of the sort.

"He got his feelings hurt, that's all," she said to the teddy bear. "It injured his pride, when he thought he had me all figured out, to discover he was wrong."

It couldn't be anything more than that, for if he really cared, he would have listened to her side of it at Brannigan's this afternoon. But instead, he had walked out. And he hadn't even tried to understand.

RACHEL HUNCHED her shoulder to hold the telephone in place while she shuffled a set of papers back into the folder. "That's all for now, Roger," she said.

"I'll do the investigation and let you know." The lawyer's voice was deep, and it rumbled pleasantly across the lines. "Is there any hurry on this one?"

"No. He won't need funds till next fall."

"That makes it easier. It might be a good idea to take things easy for a while, anyway."

Rachel didn't answer right away. Was Roger reading minds? She had been thinking herself that it might make sense to slow down a little right now, to keep from drawing attention to herself. But wasn't it odd that Roger was advising the same course of action?

"Why?" she said finally. "Are you afraid I'll overspend myself?"

The lawyer chuckled. "At the moment, I don't see how you could. But it never hurts to keep an eye on the future. I suppose it's always possible they'll stop painting cars altogether, and then where would you be?"

Rachel relaxed a little. "Not nearly as badly off as if I'd turned myself into a socialite and spent it all," she said crisply. "And I'd have a lot of good memories."

"You sound like an old lady, Rachel, looking back over a lifetime of philanthropy—not a beautiful young woman with fifty years of joy ahead of you. What I meant was that it wouldn't hurt to tuck away a little extra for yourself. It would be awfully ironic, after you've educated dozens of people, if you couldn't afford college for your own kids when the time comes."

Rachel had to grit her teeth against the sudden rush of pain caused by the image his words sent flashing through her mind—a group of small children playing on a beach. Three of them, she thought, two boys and a girl. Their heads were bent over the sand castle they were building. She couldn't see their faces, just fair skin and dark hair—skin as translucent as her own and hair as blue-black as Colin's. . . .

"Not likely," she managed to say. "In any case, I think I can hang on to enough loose change to take care of things like that." She slid the folder into its place in the bottom drawer of her desk. "Thanks, Roger, and let me know what you find out about this latest prospect."

She closed the file drawer and checked to be sure the lock had clicked. Later, if Roger's investigation showed that this young man was as good a candidate for a Carleton scholarship as Rachel thought he was, she would send all the paperwork to Roger's office in Phoenix, so there would be nothing left here except the official application. Nothing to raise suspicion that Rachel Todd might be anything more than a channel for the Carleton Fund.

It was a system that had operated beautifully for two years, ever since she'd started working with Roger. There had been lots of questions about the mysterious Carleton Fund, but in all that time, no one had figured it out. Derek had known, of course, but only because Rachel had told him—once she realized that he knew about the money. But no one had even come close to guessing the truth.

Until Colin. And now that Colin knew . . .

Well, she wasn't going to let that fact stop her from doing what she pleased. In the past three weeks, since Colin had known the truth, there had been no hint of changed attitudes toward her on campus, and there seemed to be no rumors going around. Perhaps he, like Ted Lehmann, hadn't breathed a word, after all. But she would be more cautious for a while; that was only common sense.

She was startled by a knock at her office door, and an instant later Anne Garrett popped her head in. "How about lunch?" she said. "I'd have gone through channels, but your secretary doesn't seem to be anywhere about."

Rachel hesitated. She didn't have an excuse not to go, and when things were normal there was no woman whose company she enjoyed more than Anne's. But what possible good could come out of having lunch with Colin's sister now and running the gauntlet of questions?

Of course, she reminded herself, if he had told anyone about the money, it would certainly have been Anne. And Anne knew the whole relationship had been only a show from the beginning. She wasn't going to be asking what on earth had happened, and why Rachel and Colin weren't seeing each other anymore.

"A Reuben tastes better in good company," Rachel said, pushing her unfinished work into the top drawer of her desk.

As a matter of fact, it was the first time in days that any sort of food had sounded good, and she didn't even look at the menu in the student-union dining room before ordering.

They caught up on the past couple of weeks as they waited for their food, and Rachel congratulated herself as the waitress finally set their plates down; she had managed to avoid mentioning Colin at all, and Anne hadn't even noticed.

Rachel watched in half-horrified fascination as Anne drizzled horseradish liberally over the piles of sauerkraut and corned beef on her plate. Then Anne picked up the sandwich and said, "This lunch is in the nature of a warning, actually."

Rachel paused just as she was about to bite down on her own Reuben and set it back on her plate. Her appetite had abruptly vanished. "What do you mean, warning?"

Horrible possibilities fluttered through her mind, of Colin turning to blackmail, of her whole life turning up on the front page of the *Chronicle*. No, she thought. He'd never go that far, no matter how angry he was.

"About Thanksgiving Day," Anne said easily. "I debated telling you this at all, but I thought it was only fair to let you have a chance to prepare yourself."

The tightness in Rachel's chest eased a little. "Thanksgiving? I don't think—"

"I'm getting phone calls from every branch of the family. I didn't actually keep score, but I believe almost half of them are dubious about you and can't wait to see for themselves what Colin's brought home."

"You don't need to worry about—"

"Of course, the other half want to know if they should bring clothes appropriate for a wedding—just in case."

"You're not serious."

"But, my dear, I am."

Rachel shrugged. The gesture might have looked careless, as she'd hoped, if her whole body hadn't started to tremble at that very instant. "It's just as well I'm not coming, then."

Anne dropped her Reuben. Sauerkraut splattered the front of her plaid wool suit, and she swore under her breath and reached for a napkin. "What? Why on earth not? I thought that was part of the deal."

"It...didn't work out. We had a fight, and—"

"You had a *fight?* Rachel, this whole arrangement of yours was a gag. How in heaven's name can you and

Colin have gotten into a fight over it? Never mind. I don't think I want to know.'' She sighed in exasperation. ''You mean you're just going to throw Colin to the wolves?''

Rachel bit her bottom lip. She wanted to say that calling off the plan hadn't been her idea, that Colin had made it quite clear she was no longer invited. But Anne obviously wasn't going to give her an opening.

Besides, Rachel admitted, no matter which of them had technically put a stop to the game, she was glad to be free of the obligation. She was lucky not to have to face the whole crew of McKennas and play her part once more, this time with the knowledge that if it was up to her, she would arrange things very differently indeed. She was fortunate to escape that . . . wasn't she?

Anne had hardly paused for breath. ''When the whole family realizes that the promised wonderful girl has absconded, they will give Colin no peace.''

And that's exactly what he deserved, Rachel thought. But she said meekly, ''I'm sure Colin can handle it. It was a silly idea in the first place.''

Anne looked as if she'd like to agree, but she didn't say anything.

''Besides, it couldn't go on forever,'' Rachel said, ''so everyone might as well know right now that we're not a serious item.'' She broke off a bit of her sandwich. ''I won't have time for things like that after the first of the year, anyway.''

''Your classes?''

''That's right. I just signed up for them last week, and I'm really looking forward to getting started.'' She smiled a little, trying to compensate for the absence of enthusiasm in her voice. ''I think I could enjoy being a professional student.''

Anne didn't comment, but she looked doubtful.

Rachel didn't like to face that penetrating stare, so she let her gaze drop to the sandwich Anne was holding. On one slender finger flashed an enormous solitaire diamond, at the moment almost surrounded by sauerkraut.

Before she could even stop to consider whether it was wise to ask, Rachel said, "How did you convince your husband that the newspaper wasn't the reason you wanted to marry him?"

Anne's eyebrows soared.

"Sorry," Rachel muttered. "Forget it. It's absolutely none of my business." I was an idiot to ask, she thought.

Anne said slowly, "I suppose if I'd been after the money, I'd have done it differently. For one thing, I would have been much nicer to him. At any rate, whenever you feel like talking about the wealthy man in your life, I'd love to hear the details."

Rachel opened her mouth to deny the implication and shut it again without uttering a sound. What could she say that wouldn't simply make things worse?

LATE THAT AFTERNOON, Rachel went up to Ted Lehmann's office on the top floor of the administration building. He was busy, of course, so she took a seat in the outer office and picked up a copy of Nicolet's catalog. She was plotting the sequence of classes she would need to get her doctoral degree when the door opened again and Colin came in.

She was sitting in a corner where he didn't see her right away, but she had a good view of him. His face looked thinner, she thought, and there was something missing—the quirk at the corner of his mouth that had always said, even when he wasn't actually smiling, that good humor was not far away.

He looked sad, she thought, and regret tugged at her heart—mixed with a little guilt, because she was partly responsible for making him feel that way. Then she frowned as she realized that there was another sensation, too, bubbling up from somewhere deep inside her. This one felt—incredibly—like joy. Insane as it sounded, Colin was miserable, and Rachel was happy about it.

But it took only a couple of seconds for Rachel to recognize what was really going on. She wasn't being heartless and she certainly wasn't enjoying his pain. In fact, it wasn't really happiness she was feeling, she realized, but hope. If he was no longer his usual happy-go-lucky self, that must mean he had missed her and that she had mattered to him, after all.

"Ted left this on the plane this morning," he told the secretary as he handed her a brown envelope. "I thought he'd probably need it back right away." He turned toward the door and stopped when he saw Rachel.

How could I not have realized that before, she asked herself. Why *had* Colin been so furious with her that afternoon at Brannigan's? No matter what she had done, it shouldn't have affected him so strongly. Unless . . .

If things had gone as they'd planned, they would have played out their little scene for a few more weeks and parted at Thanksgiving with no harsh feelings. With no particular feelings at all, if it came to that. So what had changed him? Rachel had fallen in love, that was true, and her developing love for him had certainly altered the balance. But that didn't explain Colin's anger.

Certainly he hadn't coveted the money. What was it Anne had said this afternoon? If she had been after her husband's money, she would have been nicer to him, that was it. The same was true of Colin; if he had suffered an attack of greed, he wouldn't have lost his temper at all. He'd have been more charming than ever.

Instead, he had practically exploded.

That doesn't mean what you'd like it to, Rachel warned herself. He said he thought we were friends, and he was hurt that I hadn't shared this with him, that's all.

But friendship could be a foundation for so much more, she thought. That was all she had wanted, anyway—the chance to see if that budding friendship could develop into something more.

Well, congratulations, Rachel. It might have even then—if you hadn't smashed it like a piece of fine china and then ground your heel into the fragments.

Ted Lehmann came out of his office. "Oh, hello, Colin."

"I brought your papers back, Ted." Colin's voice sounded stiff.

"I didn't realize I'd left them. It's awful to get old and forgetful, you know." Ted patted Colin's shoulder. "All the McKennas will be home for Thanksgiving, won't they? What will you be doing, Rachel? Dorie and I will kidnap you if you're going to be alone."

She couldn't stop herself from glancing at Colin. He was watching her silently and was obviously not going to answer for her.

Before she could decide what to say, Ted had answered his own question with a sidelong look at Colin. "That's silly of me, isn't it? Of course you'll be with the McKennas. Well, come on in. What do we need to discuss today, Rachel?"

Colin didn't move. The waiting room was not large, and Rachel had to practically brush by him. She could feel his warmth, and her skin began to quiver with the memory of how it had felt to be pressed against him, the heat of their bodies welding them together....

She wondered if Colin remembered that enchantment, too, and wished he would do something about it. With the slightest shift of his arm right now, she could be locked in his embrace and ...

He didn't move and Rachel knew he wouldn't. She also knew if there was any chance at all for the debris of their friendship to be reassembled into something worthwhile, the opening would have to come from her.

She looked at the tab of the zipper on his leather coat, a safe six inches beneath his chin, and said, "Colin, if you still want me to go to Thanksgiving dinner, I will."

The silence seemed to drag on for years.

Rachel forced herself to look up at his face. Had he even heard her? Had she spoken loudly enough? It had seemed to her she'd shouted.

He had heard; she knew from the dark shadows in his eyes.

"I did promise," she said awkwardly. "That's all I meant."

Finally Colin spoke. His voice sounded as if it belonged to someone else altogether. "I wouldn't hold you to that promise."

She nodded, accepting the verdict, and hopelessness seeped into her bones. "It's up to you, of course," she whispered, then turned toward Ted Lehmann's office.

"Rachel," he said, and she stopped. "I'll pick you up Thursday at noon."

CHAPTER TEN

THANKSGIVING DAY, the fourth Thursday in November. The day the nation sets aside each year to express its gratitude for home and hearth and family, for a good harvest and another year of work and play and freedom.

And this year, for Rachel Todd at least, it was a day of gratitude for second chances.

She would have been ready early if it hadn't been for the fact that her fingers trembled too much to easily fasten the long row of tiny gold buttons down the front of her moss-green dress. When she finally did reach the bottom, she realized she was one button off and had to start over. Not that it mattered how long she took, for the mantel clock chimed noon, and Colin did not appear.

Had he reconsidered at the last moment and decided to face the family alone, after all? Surely not. He was too much of a gentleman for that. He would at least have called her and canceled—wouldn't he?

She stepped out onto the porch to look down Waukegan Street, scolding herself for letting her impatience be so obvious. Then she realized that whatever she did could hardly matter to Colin if he didn't see it—and he wouldn't, if he wasn't coming. The idea left the pit of her stomach feeling like a black hole.

The children from the house next door came running over from their game of tag. "Mama said you were going away for Thanksgiving dinner!'' one of them cried. ''But if you're not, then you'll come and eat with us, won't you? Please?''

''What makes you think I'm not going away?'' Rachel parried.

''Because you're still here and it's time for dinner,'' the oldest declared. ''It's got to be, because Mama sent us out to play so she could finish the potatoes without us being under her feet.''

Rachel blinked away the sudden suspicious moisture in her eyes and stooped to give the child a hug. ''That's lovely of you,'' she said, ''but . . .''

From the campus, the carillon bells began to ring out the hour. Their music was pleasantly muted by distance and daytime traffic on the streets 'till the sound was little more than an echo of the midnight bells of Fall Festival.

Don't even think about the festival, Rachel ordered herself. It doesn't matter anymore. You'll learn to listen to the hours go by without letting it bother you.

The hours, she thought. But if the carillon was ringing now, that meant her mantel clock had been fast, and Colin wasn't late at all. Almost in answer, his car pulled into the driveway.

He saw her standing there, she was certain. But he sat behind the wheel for a few seconds, staring straight ahead, as if he had to brace himself for the encounter. Rachel swallowed hard and managed a hasty goodbye to the children and a wave to their mother, who had come to the door to call them in for the feast, before she stepped back into the house to get her coat. She had to lean against the door and wait a moment for her heartbeat to slow to something approaching normal before she could straighten her shoulders, lock the front door behind her and go out to meet him.

He looked taller than ever somehow, she thought, in dark gray corduroy trousers and a bulky blue-and-gray sweater. His leather coat was unzipped, and his hands were in the pockets.

"It's a beautiful day, isn't it?" she said without quite looking at him. Her voice was a little lower than usual, and she hoped that the tremor she heard was only in her imagination.

Colin looked around as if to check for himself. "I suppose it is. At least the sun's shining."

"Maybe it'll be warm this afternoon." I can't believe what I'm saying, Rachel thought. I want to throw myself at his feet and beg him to care about me, and I'm talking about the weather?

He helped her into the car, but his touch was almost impersonal. This was the kind of behavior she'd expected from him at the outset of their little plan—polite, but perfunctory—whenever no one else was around to see. To suffer it now, when she wanted so much more, cut her straight to the core.

She must have been wrong in Ted Lehmann's office that day when she thought she'd seen strain in Colin's face and allowed herself to hope it was there because he cared about her and about what happened to them. Either she had seen things that had not been there at all, or she had misinterpreted them.

Even if once upon a time he might have been starting to care, he no longer did, she told herself bluntly. She had killed any possibility of that with her own short-sightedness, and she might as well face the fact.

This was what she had sacrificed when she had not told him the truth. It had been one of the biggest mistakes of her life, she thought gloomily. And coming to a family holiday today in the hope of making things better was probably a close runner-up in the contest for worst decision of all time.

The McKennas' driveway was already full of cars, so Colin parked on the street. As they walked up the path to the house, Rachel fixed her gaze on the etched-glass panel in the front door and tried to convince herself she was not going to burst into tears.

Colin's hand brushed the nape of her neck, then his arm slid casually across her shoulders. Apparently he could feel the tension in her muscles, for he said, "It won't be so bad. You already passed all the hard tests last time."

If only that was all, Rachel thought. She had to use raw effort to keep from shrugging his arm away—not because his nearness repelled her, but because the contrast between this intimate contact and the way he had touched her when no one was watching was almost too much to bear.

Then Colin's father was at the front door to greet them, and it was too late to back out.

You'll simply have to be a good sport, Rachel, even if it kills you, because letting Colin know how much this hurts would be even worse.

"You're just in the nick of time," Professor McKenna said cheerfully. "The turkey came out of the oven five minutes ago."

"In that case, everybody get out of my way so I can go stir the gravy," Colin ordered. "Mom will be waiting for me."

In the adjoining dining room, Anne was laying napkins beside each place. "We're on to you, Colin," she warned. "It's not self-sacrifice that makes you volunteer. It's the fact that you can snitch the bits of skin off the bird."

Colin shrugged. "I have to keep up my strength somehow."

The easy humor in his voice made Rachel want to cry even more.

Under a lamp table at the corner of the room, a baby boy she hadn't seen before dropped the saucepan he'd been playing with, laboriously pushed himself to his feet and ambled across the carpet toward them. Rachel would have moved away from Colin to admire the toddler—one excuse was as good as another, and the baby was adorable—but Colin's encircling arm tightened just a little, and she found herself in the kitchen, instead, watching the final preparations.

The room smelled heavenly. The aromas of roasted turkey and freshly baked rolls mingled with the fruity scent of cranberries and the spicy fragrance of pumpkin pies. Camryn was cutting one of the pies; two other young women were dishing up food at the kitchen's center island, and both of them turned to study Rachel.

The other sisters-in-law, Rachel thought. If Anne's math was right, one of them had her doubts and the other was excited at the prospect of another wedding. She wondered which was which. Not that it mattered, she reminded herself. She would probably never see either of these young women again.

"Rachel, that's Kaye," Colin said, with a careless wave of his hand at the blond woman who was spooning mashed potatoes into a serving dish. "And the other one is Clancey." He kissed his mother's cheek and took the wire whisk out of her hand. "I'll take over now." Only Rachel saw his other hand dart out toward the turkey and surreptitiously rip off a bit of skin.

Rachel sent an uncertain smile at the two women and turned to Colin's mother. There was some comfort in knowing that Kathleen McKenna, at least, was blithely oblivious to the currents in the room. "May I help?"

"I could use a hand getting the turkey from the roaster and out of Colin's reach so he can concentrate on the gravy," Kathleen murmured.

Colin looked so wounded that Rachel had to smile. She steadied the roaster while Kathleen lifted out the enormous bird, and held her breath till it was safely on a huge china platter. Then she sniffed appreciatively. "He's picture-perfect, Kathleen. How do you get it so evenly brown?"

"Oh, turkey's easy." Kathleen moved the platter to the center island.

"That's what she always says," Colin murmured. He put the roaster on top of the stove and began stirring the drippings. The position of his body effectively blocked Rachel into the corner of the kitchen. She wondered if he realized how very cozy they must look.

No doubt, she thought. He probably planned it that way.

"It's true," Kathleen said. "A turkey takes so little attention that it's one of the few things I do really well in the kitchen. I just start it in a hot oven for the first hour and baste it with butter every thirty minutes to get that nice golden glow."

"One Christmas she forgot to set the oven timer and didn't baste the bird at all," Colin added. "It tasted all right, but we called it Paleface. And then there was the time she forgot—"

"Keep stirring," his mother recommended, "or we'll never let you live down the lumpy gravy."

Rachel saw the gleam of mischief spring to life in his eyes as he shot a glance at his mother, and her heart ached. Would she ever again see that gleam when he looked at her?

The Thanksgiving table looked like a Norman Rockwell painting, Rachel thought as they assembled in the dining room a little later. At the head of the table, the turkey, still steaming gently, occupied the place of honor in front of Dennis McKenna. There was scarcely a square inch of tablecloth showing under the masses of food.

Dennis looked down the table, past the faces of young adults, elderly relatives and babies in high chairs, to his wife. He cleared his throat. "Kath, do you ever feel that we're responsible for an awful lot of people?" He didn't wait for an answer, but put out one hand, palm up, to Rachel, who was seated to his right. The other he extended to Colin's grandmother, sitting to his left, right across the table from Rachel.

When the circle of linked hands was complete all around the table, including the smallest of the babies, Dennis bowed his head. "This is a day to reflect with soberness, as well as with joy, on all our many blessings," he said softly. "Good health and bounty, good friends—"

"Five children who all speak to each other," Kathleen murmured, and there was a ripple of laughter around the table.

"And the new children they have brought to us," Dennis added. "The grown-up ones . . ."

He squeezed Rachel's hand just a little as he said it. Something deep inside her tightened into a hard knot. She was glad she was looking at her plate just then and not at Colin. It was difficult enough to sit there quietly beside the man she loved and hold his hand.

"And of course the four of the next generation," Dennis went on. "For all these things we are most truly—"

"Daddy," Anne interrupted plaintively. "We all expect Mother to be a little vague when it comes to numbers. But when you lose count, I start worrying."

Dennis frowned. He let go of Rachel's hand and pointed at each child, counting aloud. "I still get four. Of course, I'm counting the baby that's on the way, if that's what—"

"So am I," Anne said demurely. "And I count five."

All eyes were on her now, and Rachel noted with interest that Anne had turned ever so slightly pink.

"Early August," Anne said, ducking her head almost shyly. "She'll be a Leo, poor child."

"The horseradish," Rachel murmured. "I ought to have guessed there was something unusual going on, the way you were squirting that stuff around at lunch the other day."

Over the initial congratulations, Colin said, "What do you mean, 'she'? It could be a boy, Anne."

Anne shook her heard. "I absolutely refuse to have a boy."

"Children," Dennis began, "this is not the time—"

"I don't see what difference it would make," Grandmother Nell grumbled. "Any girl of yours will be as much of a tomboy as you ever were, Anne."

Dennis sighed.

"So much for saying grace," Colin muttered. He let Rachel's hand slip out of his. "In the last fifteen years, Dad's never once made it to an 'Amen' before we all break into an argument of one kind or another."

Dennis, too, seemed to have given up the idea of properly finishing his prayer of thanks. He reached for the carving knife and fork, then very deliberately set them down again. "If there are any more announcements," he suggested, "why don't we get them over with now, before I pick up a deadly weapon? I'd hate to get a shock while I was carving."

He didn't look at Rachel, but she could feel the accumulated weight of what seemed a thousand pairs of eyes. For one insane moment she actually contemplated standing up and saying, "Yes, I have an announcement you'll all be interested in. I'm in love with Colin, and I'd marry him in a minute...."

Except that not every person at the table would be thrilled. One of them would be horrified.

Rachel stared at her napkin and willed herself not to change color.

Beside her, Colin shrugged. "No announcements, I guess," he said easily. "You might as well carve, Dad."

The talk turned back to Anne's news, and the heckling carried them through dinner. Rachel even regained her composure enough to get a few remarks in.

As she helped to clear the table after dessert, she wasn't surprised to fine Anne giving her a mock-reproachful look as she stacked china. "Foolish me," Anne accused. "I actually thought you'd be grateful to me for taking the pressure off you, Rachel."

"With your announcement? You mean you planned it that way?"

"Of course I did. And wasn't my timing perfect? Or didn't you even notice that no one was nagging you about a wedding date? Of course you didn't. You were too busy badgering me right along with the rest."

Everyone pitched in to clean up the mess, and in less than an hour the kitchen was quiet again. The babies had been carried off for naps, and the rest of the family gravitated toward the big living room, where a parade was just starting on television.

Rachel was the last one into the room. She'd planned it that way so she could simply curl up in a corner or drop onto the floor. If she did it casually, no one would pay any attention to the fact that she was staying as far from Colin as possible.

But he had staked out a place on the long couch, and as she came in he moved just enough to leave a space for her, patting the cushion beside him.

If she had ignored him then, it would have been painfully obvious to all. She took a deep breath and sat down beside him. Almost automatically, it seemed, he turned her slightly so her back rested against his shoulder, and draped both arms around her.

And then he proceeded to ignore her completely and focus his entire attention on the parade.

She sat there as if paralyzed. His chest rose and fell against her spine in a soft hypnotic rhythm until she found her breathing synchronized with his. His arms formed a warm cage, imprisoning her, and his voice, when he spoke at all, tickled her ear.

She felt like a kettle of water held above a flame that was slowly and inexorably being turned higher. A whistling kettle, at that, for sooner or later she would break into a boil and begin to scream.

Could Colin possibly be unaware of how being this close to him was affecting her?

Of course he could, she told herself. It wasn't affecting him at all. The electrical field he was generating might be sending tiny rhythmic shocks through her bones, but it was doing nothing to him.

To her relief, the parade was a short one, and as soon as a football game took its place, the McKenna women moved back to the kitchen.

Just get up and follow them, Rachel told herself. It's easy enough.

But it wasn't. It might be torture to sit there next to Colin, but tearing herself away, knowing she would probably never be so close to him again, wasn't easy, either.

Ultimately she managed to get to her feet, and she walked into the kitchen just as Clancey said, "Because I'm not ready to start a family, that's why. And I don't care what science says, I'm bringing bottled water when I come for Christmas—just in case this thing about babies turns out to be a virus in the drinking water."

"If that's what's causing it," Camryn said sweetly, "it's probably too late to do you any good. But you might suggest caution to Rachel, just in case."

Rachel felt herself turning beet red.

Anne bit her lip hard, obviously trying to strangle a laugh. Her eyes were dancing, but her voice was sober. "As long as we're talking about Christmas, shouldn't we draw names for the gift exchange?"

"I knew we were forgetting something," Camryn said. "Hand me that little pad of paper and I'll start." She began tearing off sheets and writing names on each. Then she looked up at Rachel. "This is a terribly tactless question, I realize," she said, "but shall I put your name in?"

Rachel's hand tightened on the edge of the butcherblock island until she thought her knuckles would snap. "No," she said quietly. "I'll be going away."

Camryn nodded. "Going back to spend the holiday with your family in Arizona?" she asked. "Lucky girl, to get away where it's warm."

Anne's eyes were full of warm concern and reflected pain.

She knows there's no one, Rachel thought. I hope that's all she's thinking.

Anne started to speak, but then her gaze shifted over Rachel's shoulder and she shrugged, instead, and began folding up the slips of paper and dropping them into a small bowl.

Behind Rachel, Colin said, "Anyone for a fast game of Scrabble?"

"If you don't mind, I'd like to go home soon," Rachel said. She hardly recognized her own voice. She forced herself to look at him.

He seemed to read the desperation in her eyes. "Of course. Whatever you like."

Rachel's goodbyes took the very last of her energy. It was difficult to be casual and careless when she knew quite well that, barring accidental encounters, she would not see these people again.

Anne gave her a hug and whispered, "I'm sorry. I didn't realize until just now.... Are you all right?"

Rachel managed to nod. Even Anne, she thought, she would not seek out again; much as she liked the young woman, now that Anne knew how much she cared, Rachel couldn't face the explanations. And even if they once got past all that, building a friendship with Colin's sister would only increase the pain as time went on.

Rachel slumped in the front seat of Colin's car. He didn't even look at her.

"Well, that's over," she said inanely.

Colin didn't answer, but a few minutes later, as he stopped the car outside her house, he said slowly, "Where will you go for Christmas, Rachel?"

She wasn't sure she'd heard him right. "What?"

"You said you were going away. Where?"

Rachel shrugged. "I don't know. It doesn't matter."

His hands tightened on the wheel as if he was struggling with himself. Finally, awkwardly, he said, "It's a terrible time to be alone. You'd be very welcome—"

"No, thanks." She realized how bitter the refusal must sound and tried to soften it. "It's much better if we stick to the original deal. You're going to have a hard enough time explaining the whole thing—except that somehow I don't think we were very convincing today.''

He nodded. ''I suspect you're right.''

She tried to sound cheerful. ''Well, that ought to make it easier for you in the long run. Thank you, Colin. It was a very nice holiday.''

She saw him move and braced herself for his touch. But he only caught a coppery curl and let it slide sinuously between his fingers. Then the back of his hand brushed softly against her cheek and he said, ''Goodbye, Rachel—and joy be with you.''

It had almost the sound of a benediction, and she knew she'd heard it before. But it took a moment to remember that the phrase was from one of the Irish folk songs they had shared at Brannigan's that first time.

She ducked her head so he wouldn't see the tears in her eyes and forced herself to smile. ''Goodbye, Colin. Don't walk me to the house...please.'' Her voice almost broke on the last word. She pushed the car door open and hurried up the drive.

Joy be with you... The truth was, joy would never be hers again—or at any rate, not the sort of joy she had glimpsed when she was with him, the sort of joy she could have known forever if only he could love her as she loved him.

Rachel stumbled into the house. Bandit uncurled from his favorite spot on the rocking chair and eyed her warily. Desperate for some kind of living contact, Rachel scooped the cat up in her arms.

Now that it was finally safe to cry, the tears wouldn't come—only dry racking sobs that shook her body till she could hardly stand. She felt as if she had been whipped from head to toe.

She had given the front door a push, but not hard enough to close it properly. She didn't realize that until Colin said, "What on earth . . . ?"

Her hands tightened on the cat's soft body until Bandit yowled in protest. In three quick steps Colin was across the room beside her—but he did not comfort her. He simply lifted the cat out of her arms. "What is it, Rachel?"

She shook her head wordlessly.

Colin sighed. "You don't trust anybody, do you? If you were invited to join a vocal quartet, you'd insist on singing all four parts yourself."

Rachel tensed. There was something in his voice. . . .

Colin put Bandit down on the rocking chair and stood for a moment stroking him. He didn't look at Rachel. "I'm sorry. It's not my place to criticize you." He turned toward the door.

Her voice was high and strained. "You think I don't trust you?"

"Rachel, it's as plain as . . ."

She shook her head violently.

Colin sighed. "You think I'm just like Derek, don't you? You even asked if I was having second thoughts about passing up the opportunity to get all your money."

"No," she said. "You're not like Derek. Not at all. Derek could never have hurt me the way you have."

He looked stunned.

Rachel felt as if a dam had burst somewhere inside her, and she could no longer stop herself. "I don't know why I should trust you, Colin," she said bitterly. "I've had no experience in my life with men who can be trusted. . . ." Her voice broke, and hot painful tears began to flow.

Colin said something under his breath she didn't quite catch. Then he put both arms around her and pulled her down with him into the big chair by the fireplace, cradling her like a baby while she sobbed out her pain.

Finally the flood of tears died to a trickle, and the racking sobs settled down to a hiccup now and then. She was warm in his arms, it was peaceful there, and she didn't want to move ever again.

"Want to tell me about it?" he said.

She nodded, her face was still buried against the damp shoulder of his sweater. And she meant it, too; she did want to tell him. She just didn't seem to know how to start.

"Derek, of course," Colin prompted. "I wondered if there wasn't something more. Abuse?"

"Only the kind you saw. And even that didn't start till after he found out I wasn't going to turn everything over to him."

Colin twisted a copper curl around his finger. "Your father, then? The marvelous man who left you all the money. Surely he..."

"He didn't, actually. Leave it to me, I mean." Rachel, with her head burrowed into his shoulder, felt the very instant his body tightened and he began to pull away.

"If you're going to change your story again, Rachel..."

"No." Her voice was shaky with the effort of trying to make him understand. "It was his money, of course. It's just that he didn't arrange for me to have it. He didn't even make a will. I got the money simply because I was the only relative they could find."

"You mean he'd forgotten about you?"

"No. I mean he knew perfectly well I existed and exactly how to find me." Her voice was flat. "He simply didn't care, Colin." She was shivering again, and Colin pulled her closer.

"Oh, Rachel." His fingertips traced the hollow of her cheek.

"I went to Arizona because I knew he was there." She told him, her voice level and precise, about her search and her move across the country and the way she had so carefully planned her first meeting with Henry Todd because she knew what a shock it would be for him.

"But I didn't expect what a shock it would be for me," she finished almost bitterly. "I guess I expected some sort of fairy tale—the long-lost princess finds her lonely old father, and he welcomes her with tears and rapture and they live happily ever after. Well, in this case..."

Colin's arms tightened around her.

"It's funny, I suppose," she mused. "I put off contacting him for months. It was as if something deep inside me knew he didn't want me. And when I finally went to see him, and he said that as far as he was concerned he'd never had a daughter, and he certainly didn't need or want one now..."

"It's all right," Colin whispered. "It's over. It was his loss, Rachel, and his shame. Not yours."

But she scarcely heard him. "I didn't want the money," she said. "It's dirty money. If he'd made a will and left me a hundred dollars, I'd have treasured it, because at least I'd have known he was thinking of me, just me, at the end. But millions don't mean anything, not when there's no love to go with it."

Rachel felt a fresh surge of tears, and she bit her lip to get control of herself. "For the first entire year, because of that, I wouldn't spend even a penny on myself. Derek thought I was insane." She laughed harshly. "But then, he also thought I was insane to give the better portion of it away, when it could buy me a wonderful guy like him."

Colin stroked her hair, and after a long time, he said quietly, "And I didn't understand why you felt you had to protect yourself. All I could see was that you'd lied to me."

Rachel raised her head. "I would have told you, Colin. I was starting to tell you, that day at Brannigan's, when Peggy dropped her news."

"And I went berserk," he said wryly.

"When you accused me of all those things—hiding out and lying and trying to protect my money—I was hurt, too. I wasn't doing those things. Not deliberately, at any rate. I hadn't told you about the money because it *didn't matter*. We were friends—truly we were. That's what I want again, Colin. Please, can we be friends?"

He sighed, but he didn't say anything at all, and suddenly Rachel was afraid. Had anything changed, after all? Or was she still stuck in that same hopeless morass, except that now Colin knew exactly how she felt? That helpless plea for friendship had been the biggest lie she'd ever told. Did he know it, and feel sorry for her?

"Why did you come back just now, anyway?" she asked cautiously.

He smiled a little. "I'd forgotten to give Bandit his Thanksgiving present." He reached for his jacket, discarded on the floor beside the couch, and pulled a big bag of plastic straws from the pocket.

In her entire life, Rachel had never felt so humiliated. He had come back to deliver a simple gift, and she had sobbed all over him and subjected him to her life story.

"I see," she said flatly, and started to draw away from him.

He wouldn't let her go. "It was a tremendous shock that day at Brannigan's when I realized how much of yourself you'd been hiding. It was all so obvious, once

I realized that nothing about you made sense if I looked at it any other way."

"Colin—"

"Hush a minute and listen. All I could see was what a fool I had been to let you pull that on me. You see, I was going to propose to you that day."

Rachel's eyes filled with tears. "And then...you didn't want to anymore, did you?"

"I was so stunned I didn't know what I wanted. And even if I had known, what would you have thought? That I was after the money?"

"No." It was only a whisper.

"I thought it was obvious that we belonged together—the fun we had and the way you reacted to me. I guess I thought that because I had always known how special and beautiful you were, you should be able to read my mind and know how much I loved you—my bright, funny, lovely, unpredictable Rachel."

"Especially unpredictable," she muttered.

Colin nodded. "I think the reason I was so furious you hadn't told me was that I suddenly believed perhaps you didn't have any feelings for me at all, and you were simply a better actress than I had given you credit for being. I thought you saw no reason to let me get close, let me share the hidden things in your life."

She raised her hand to caress his cheek. Her fingertips were trembling. "Is that why you were so cold in Ted Lehmann's office that day? And today, when we were alone?"

He nodded. "I was longing to get my hands on you—and afraid of what would happen if I did. So when everyone was watching and you couldn't turn around and slap me, I took advantage of it, knowing it would be the last time I dared to touch you. You didn't mind?"

"I minded," she admitted huskily. "I hated thinking that you didn't want to touch me." She pulled away from him, just a little, with her hands still clasped at the nape of his neck. "Explain one thing to me, Colin. You had to brace yourself before you could even come up to the house this morning. Don't deny it. I could see it."

"Don't you know why? You were standing on the porch surrounded by kids, and I couldn't help thinking how much I'd like for those to be my kids gathered around you. My family, waiting for me."

"Oh," Rachel said softly. "Yes, I can see that." She realized that his eyes had begun to glow, and she added hastily, "I mean, I understand, Colin, not that I'm making plans!"

"Really?" His voice was gruff. "It sounds like creative visualization to me—and I'm all for it."

His kisses had always aroused her, but the one he gave her now allowed her glimpses of what lay ahead—a lifetime secure in the knowledge of his love. By the time he stopped kissing her, Rachel was too shattered even to think of moving. She put her head down on his shoulder and dreamily listened to the beat of his heart against her ear. "Funny," she murmured. "Both of us caught in our own brilliant idea like flies in a web."

"Well...not exactly." He sounded a little uneasy, and Rachel raised her head and looked at him with suspiciously narrowed eyes.

"I was sunk from the beginning," he confessed. "The very beginning, I mean. The day I took you and Ted to Minneapolis."

Rachel's eyes widened. "What? You're not going to try to convince me you fell in love at first sight, are you?"

"Well, maybe it wasn't quite that fast. All I knew is that I wanted to get to know you a whole lot better—and that you were so oblivious it was a waste of time to try."

"I didn't even see you, I suppose," Rachel admitted.

"That, my love, was painfully apparent. I was trying to get your attention, and you obviously thought I was not your type. It wasn't until the night of the thunderstorm at the ice-cream parlor that I realized you weren't turned off by *me,* necessarily. You just had no interest in men at all."

"You don't need to make it sound so awful."

Colin grinned. "Hey, I'm not complaining. It kept you free till you met me, didn't it? Then you made your crazy proposition, and I thought if the only way to get your attention was to take part in your damn-fool plot—"

"—then you'd oblige me."

"My pleasure. I was brought up to be agreeable to ladies."

Her voice rose. "You're a schemer, Colin McKenna!"

"That surprises you, my love?"

He kissed her again, long and thoroughly, and Rachel's momentary irritation faded away. What, after all, did she have to be upset about? It was pretty flattering, actually.

"About the money, Colin . . ." she said finally.

He held her a little distance from him and looked down into her eyes. "I don't want to know the details. And I don't care whether you buy college educations with it or bury it in the back yard or fling bags of cash off the top of the Empire State Building. All right?"

She smiled a little. "Well, I'm going to do some of each, I think. What you said about hiding out and lying to protect the money . . ."

"I'm sorry for saying that."

"Don't be. There was some truth to it. That's why I was in Ted's office that day. I thought he could help me figure out how to stop hiding, without actually making any big splashes, either. It's going to take some time for me to be comfortable with that, Colin, but I'm going to try."

"Let me know if I can help, all right? Otherwise, I'll stay out of it." He began running his fingers through her curls in a soothing rhythm. "In the meantime, Rachel Todd, are you still going away for Christmas?"

"Doesn't look like it, does it?" she said softly.

He chuckled. "No, it doesn't. And we'd better decide on a wedding date soon—unless you like the idea of being hounded about it by my family all through the Christmas holidays."

Rachel smiled. "The sooner the better, Colin." Suddenly she sat upright and said, "Anne's going to be shocked."

"You can say that again."

There was a tinge of laughter in his voice, and Rachel looked at him curiously.

"Hadn't you figured her out yet?" Colin asked. "I was the extra man she was trying to set you up with at her dinner party that night."

Rachel's mouth fell open. "That rotten little sneak."

"Not that she had any luck, poor girl. You said you didn't have an escort, so she started looking for me. But by the time she tracked me down, I told her I couldn't come because I already had a date that night. With you, but of course Anne didn't know that. Then you called her up to say you were bringing a man, after all...."

Rachel gave a gurgle of laughter. "No wonder she looked so shocked when you walked in. She deserved it for trying to set me up with a blind date."

"Well, half-blind, maybe," Colin pointed out. "Don't forget that I'd have known exactly what I was getting into."

Rachel frowned. "You said you were going bowling with the boys."

"No. That was later, after you'd invited me to the party. And what I said was I *could* have gone bowling that night, not that I'd been intending to."

Rachel pretended to think that over. "Hmm. I guess there's no point in holding a grudge about it."

"Certainly not," Colin murmured. "There are so many more interesting things to do." He pulled her back into his arms, and the light she had seen so often in his eyes sprang to life again. This time it was like a candle flame catching and glowing. But now she knew what it was—a mixture of passion and humor and tenderness. It was the light of love.

And he whispered, as his mouth brushed hers, "Don't let me forget to put a little bottle of jet fuel in your stocking at Christmastime. Just in case you feel like dabbing some behind your ears now and then."